Sure 'Lock
CLAW & WARDER
Episode 8

Erik Henry Vick

RATATOSKR PUBLISHING

NEW YORK

Copyright © 2020 by **Erik Henry Vick**

All rights reserved. No part of this publication may be reproduced, distributed or transmitted in any form or by any means, without prior written permission.

Ratatoskr Publishing
2080 Nine Mile Point Road, Unit 106
Penfield, NY 14526

Publisher's Note: This is a work of fiction. Names, characters, places, and incidents are a product of the author's imagination. Locales and public names are sometimes used for atmospheric purposes. Any resemblance to actual people, living or dead, or to businesses, companies, events, institutions, or locales is completely coincidental.

Sure 'Lock/ Erik Henry Vick. -- 1st ed.
ISBN 978-1-951509-10-1

TABLE OF CONTENTS

Chapter 1 1
Chapter 2 29
Chapter 3 181
Chapter 4 257
Chapter 5 263
AUTHOR'S NOTE 269
ABOUT THE AUTHOR 273

For those of you who spend your lives taking care of others.

I hope you enjoy *Sure 'Lock*. If so, please consider joining my Readers Group—details can be found at the end of the last chapter.

Chapter 1

The Body

In the magical justice system, magically based offenses are considered bad form.

In the Locus of New York, the dedicated teams of supernatural detectives who investigate these breaches of Canon and Covenants are members of an elite squad known as the Supernatural Inquisitors Squad.

These are their stories.

I

Wendy Harrison-Green rubbed her face and grimaced down at her little poochkins. Little Dee was as demanding as any diva and twice as imperious as any prima donna. She didn't care a whit that it was before six in the morning. She didn't notice the pea-soup fog that shrouded DeWitt Clinton Park. She didn't mind dragging Wendy outdoors into the cold when all sane people remained inside, warm under the covers, dreaming good dreams. She still demanded *exactly* the right spot to do her business—not too close to any other dog's territory, not too far from the planting beds, although certainly not in them, at least three steps from the concrete path, yet not more than eleven. She didn't seem to know that in DeWitt Clinton Park, such criteria excluded, well, *everywhere*.

So, around and around Little Dee dragged her. Sniffing, taking a hesitant step or two, lifting her paws off the dew-drenched grass and shaking them, sniffing again, turning her head, then trotting right back on the path, whining and looking up at her as though she were the recalcitrant one.

"Come on, come on," crooned Wendy. "Just pick a spot, Lil Dee." They rounded the curved western-most path for the third time and started toward the handball courts—human shivering from the sudden cold, poodle walking with her nose in the air as though to chastise Wendy for rushing her.

A horrible noise thrummed from over toward the ball field—or maybe toward the dog run. As loud as one of the Seven Angels blowing one of the Seven Trumpets, the noise drifted down through the registers from hellish shriek to hateful snarl.

Little Dee sprinted closer, charging between Wendy's ankles, then standing there shivering, gaze darting about like an insane pixie's. "There, there," said Wendy. "But *you're* supposed to be protecting *me*, Lil Dee."

From the same direction as the snarling shout, a man screamed.

Shuddering, Wendy scooped Little Dee into her arms, backing away from the sound—which, as it happened, was directly between her and her home on West 52nd Street.

The fog swirled and danced, netherworld shadow creatures forming, looming, disappearing in seconds, replaced by some other underworld nightmare. Wendy darted a glance over her shoulder, but there was no retreat there—only 12th Avenue and the piers beyond it.

The brush and trees swayed with an unfelt wind, and footsteps padded closer and closer, their maker hidden by the fog. Little Dee whined in her arms, and the poodle's bladder let loose, spilling hot urine down the front of Wendy's robe. "Well, isn't that just *marvelous?*" she hissed, holding the little dog away from her chest.

The fog swirled, then seemed to freeze and glowed a flickering yellow-orange, as though someone stood within it and burned with hellish flames. A low growl rumbled from the lumpy, grey-cotton wall of mist, and Wendy backed away, ducking behind a tree trunk.

She stood there, her back to the trunk, heart beating like crazy, barely breathing, barely *thinking.* Little Dee had gone tharn with terror—nothing more than a statue. Footfalls padded onto the concrete pad, accompanied by a clicking noise similar to that made by Little Dee's nails. Wendy gathered her courage and peeked around the trunk.

A two-headed black dog stood on the path, one nose up in the air, tasting the wind, and the other held low, lips curled back from its fangs, gaze peering into the same fog that shrouded the beast. Flame flickered from the creature's fur and danced in its eye sockets. Glowing triangular claws tipped each paw.

Wendy slapped her hand over her mouth to stifle a gasp and turned away, putting her shoulder blades against the rough bark, mouthing silent prayers that the hound wouldn't sense her.

After a moment, the sound of the hound's footfalls drew past and on toward 12th Avenue, then faded out of audible range. Wendy stood stock-still for a long time afterward, her dog's now-cold urine seeping through her robe and gown and making her skin clammy and gross, and, for once, Little Dee didn't squirm, didn't whine, didn't complain.

Wendy waited and waited, then finally summoned the courage and stepped out of her hiding place. The hound was gone, though she could still see its charred footprints on the concrete. She followed them, moving away from the direction the beast had gone, tracing its backtrail until she nearly tripped over the body.

Her scream echoed through the early morning stillness, as rough and intrusive as the hound's snarl.

2

Dru put the Crown Vic in park, killed the engine, then turned and cast an assessing glance at Leery. "It's too soon," she said quietly.

"Nonsense," said Leery. "It's early. I always look like death-warmed-over this early."

"No, you don't," said Dru, but then she sighed. "I know you want to get back to work, Leery, but it's only been seven weeks since Agon—"

"Yeah," said Leery. "Seven weeks of the best medical care I could ever hope for. Seven weeks of blessings and healing magic from both Gehenna and...other places, thanks to Puriel. Seven weeks of enforced convalescence, of eating right, of watching Luci channel more power through my body than I've seen expended in my lifetime." He looked her in the eye. "Am I in perfect shape?" He shook his head slowly. "No, but I can't get back into shape without working. I've gone as far as I can resting."

"Okay," she said, looking down at her hands wrestling in her lap.

"Dru, I'm okay. I'm ready for this."

"Okay," she repeated, but she didn't look up, didn't smile.

"I know you're worried. I'll tell you what. I'll follow your lead in this case. You take point, I'll hang back."

"Okay," she said once more. "But, Leery?"

"Yeah?"

"I don't want to be saved if it means you're…" She swallowed hard, and her hands attacked one another with more vigor.

"Hey," Leery began, but for once, he had no witty rejoinder, no joke, no pun to offer her. "If it comes to that, I'll call for help."

"Promise?" she asked.

"Yeah. The people I can call on for help can handle anything, right?"

She lifted her chin and let it drop, then, without looking at him, she opened her door and got out. "If you get tired, say something, okay?"

Leery got out of the passenger side and saluted her with his Starbucks cup. "Yeah, I'll order a Starbucks and rest up." He grinned. "Now, quit worrying. We've got a body to paw over and a killer to sniff out."

"Dog park," Dru said with a smile. "You'll be right at home." She led him across the street and into DeWitt Clinton Park, taking the concrete path to the dog run, which crime scene lights lit up despite the thick fog.

Two uniformed sergeants stood next to the crime scene tape marking off the area. Leery strolled up, a smile on his face.

"Hey, there Logsdon. Zackheim." He nodded to each officer. "Must be important to get both of you down here before the crack of dawn. What gives?"

"I'll tell you, Oriscoe," said Logsdon. "The guy back there over my shoulder isn't taking a nap. He's dead, see? Dog got him."

"Or a wolf. And he's a high-powered Wall Street magister." Zackheim nodded to Dru and stuck out his hand. "Ben Zackheim."

"Dru Nogan," she said and shook his hand.

"This high-powered Wall Street magister have a name?" asked Leery.

SURE 'LOCK   9

Logsdon shoved the clipboard at him. "Sign in. You know the drill." He turned to Dru. "John Logsdon," he said.

"Delighted," she said.

"His name's Richard Brook," said Zackheim.

"Of that fancy firm across from the Exchange? Brook, Merris, and Myercough?" asked Leery.

"Yeah," said Logsdon, "but it's not Myercough."

"It's Myer," said Zackheim, and then he coughed.

"What? Not Myercough? Just Myer? I could have sworn—"

"You're not listening, Oriscoe. It's Myer—" Logsdon coughed. "Get it? Myer—" He coughed again.

"Oh. He's a goblin I take it?"

"Yep," said Zackheim.

"Speaking of which, where are your little gobo friends? Boob and Whatsit?"

"Bob and Lou!" came a growl from the fog-shrouded trees. "Watch your ass, poodle, or you might find my foot in it. And it wasn't a dog or a wolf. That was a Hell Hound."

"Dammit, Bob!" said another goblin voice from the gloom. "The princess probably doesn't like that kind of talk."

"Yeah, Boob," said Leery. "We call those creatures Barghests in Gehenna."

"*We*, mutt? You got a mouse in your pocket or what?"

Leery grinned and scrawled his signature on the clipboard. "Glad to know some things never change."

Dru signed in, then held the tape up so Leery didn't have to bend much. Even so, he winced ducking under it. "See you around, fellas," he said in a strained voice.

"Right," said Logsdon and Zackheim at the same time.

"Not if we see you first, Alpo-breath," growled the fog.

Leery lifted a hand and waved, a smile plastered on his lips. "I love those little fellows. It's nice to know they aren't all monsters, goblins," he said under his breath. "Especially after all that mess with the Redcaps."

"Uh-huh," said Dru, her gaze already on the sheet-draped body lying in the center of the dog park. A woman stood off to the side, dressed in a stained housecoat and holding a toy poodle. "Witness?" she whispered.

"Looks like it."

SURE 'LOCK 11

Liz Hendrix stood near the head of the body, writing in a spiral notebook and grimacing at the fog. "Look what the cat dragged back from Gehenna," she said as they approached. "You sure you should be up and around so soon?"

"Hey, get in line," said Oriscoe. "The worrywart line starts with Dru, then my daughters, Lucifer, Agrat, Lieutenant Van Helsing, Vinny Gonofrio, Puriel, Evie—"

"Oh, you wish," said Liz. "Maybe—and I'm stressing the maybe here, Oriscoe—maybe Dru."

"Oh, that hurts, Hendrix. That hurts." He walked over to the body and stooped with a grimace and groan. "So, what do we have here?" He took the corner of the white sheet and lifted it, peering at the mauled man beneath. "Some kind of wild animal?"

"According to your witness, it was a two-headed dog." Liz glanced over her shoulder, then leaned forward. "Though I think she might have a few screws loose in her belfry. She says the two-headed dog was on fire but didn't seem to burn."

"A Hel—" Leery cut his gaze toward Dru. "A, um, Barghest? In a park in Hel's Kitchen? This ain't the Snickelways."

Liz shrugged. "I've heard of stranger things."

"Me, too," said Leery. "I love that show."

Liz shook her head and looked at Dru. "Not even a brush with death served up by a dragon can improve his humor."

"I'm not sure there's enough power in all the Nine Realms to effect such a change in the fabric of the universe."

Leery groaned as he straightened. "Jealousy, ladies, is such a cruel master." He hooked his thumb at the shrouded body. "Anything he can tell us?"

Liz shook her head. "His soul has departed."

"Carried off by the Barghest?" asked Dru.

"That's the most likely scenario."

"Would Hinton know?" asked Leery.

"I doubt it," said Liz. "If the Barghest carried the soul away, it's lost to us."

"Then we'll have to track down this Barghest via other means," said Leery. "Anyone have a dog treat?"

"Why? You hungry?" asked Liz.

"Har, har," said Leery. "Come on, Dru, let's—"

"Before you go far, this guy's partners are on their way down to the Two-Seven for a briefing and to give a statement if you need it. They wanted to come here, but I said no."

"Smart, Hendrix," said Leery.

"Right," said Liz with a shrug. "I figured you wouldn't want them ogling the body."

"Want to give us a preliminary COD?"

"Sure, Leery. Let's go with dog-bite."

"Cute, Hendrix. Real cute."

"Aren't I just?" she said with a smile. "But it's still a Barghest bite that caused his death."

3

Leery and Dru got off the elevator and walked into the squad room. Two dapper magisters—one human, one goblin—sat waiting in Van Helsing's office, and she waved them in.

"Morning, Lieu," said Leery. "Can I get anyone a coffee?"

The human magister stood and offered his hand. "Harland Merris," he said. "This is Vastalan Myer"—he covered his mouth with his free hand and coughed—"and we are Richard Brook's business partners."

"Leery Oriscoe. This beauty is my partner, Dru Nogan. And you *were* Richard Brook's partners."

Merris nodded to Dru as he shook Leery's hand. For his part, Myercough sneered and looked toward the opposite corner of the room.

"I hope you're not expecting much," said Leery. "We've come directly from the scene, but there wasn't much there."

"Figured as much," grunted Myercough. "It's no wonder you ended up ruining Slypinch's career by mistake."

"Uh..." began Dru.

"Don't mind him," said Merris. "He's been grumpy since forever." He smiled. "What can you share with us about poor Richard?"

"He's dead, for one thing," said Leery.

"You don't say?" asked Myercough with a churlish sneer.

"Hey, you wouldn't happen to have a red hat at home, would you? You seem awfully upset about what happened to your corrupt pal."

"A red hat? A Redcap, you mean?" Myercough's smile was predatory and vicious. "I wonder how many lawsuits I can file based off that one slight?"

"Relax, Vast," said Harland Merris. "You started it, after all."

"Started it?" growled the goblin. "Started it? Hardly!"

"Gentlemen, please," said Epatha Van Helsing. "Let's stick to the case in front of us. We don't need any dust-ups over what's past."

"What can you tell us about Richard Brook?" asked Dru.

"He and I formed the firm seventeen years ago," said Harland. "Richard and I, I mean. Vast joined us, what? Twelve years ago, Vast?"

"Yes."

"What kind of junk is your firm concerned with? I've always wondered what made Wall Street firms hop."

"Money, Detective, and lots of it," hissed Vastalan Myercough.

Merris chuckled. "We are the senior partners of Brook, Merris, and Myer"—again, he covered his mouth and coughed—"Detective. Our firm employs one hundred seventy-nine magisters, and each and every one of them is tasked with ensuring our clients get the best deals possible. We do public offerings, private placements, mergers, acquisitions, and the like."

"Oh, so like stocks and stuff?"

"That's right, Detective," said Myercough. "Stocks and stuff." He sneered as he said it.

"Oh. Neato," said Leery. "Maybe you can give an old dog a few tips."

"Hardly," said Myercough. "We are—"

"He's teasing you, Vastalan," said Merris, looking at Leery askance. "I believe he's a lot smarter than he's pretending to be."

Leery wagged his eyebrows at Dru. "Caught, again."

"Was Mr. Brook working on anything big? Something that might...I don't know..." Dru shrugged.

"Cause someone to want to murder him?" asked Merris with a chuckle. "We deal in paper, Detectives. Contracts. Deal offerings. Things of that nature. Dry, boring paperwork."

"But we're talking about deals like when one corporate giant buys another company, then ruins all the employees' lives, right?"

Myercough chuckled. "Not as dumb as he looks, eh, Harland?"

"Any deal could look like that to an outsider, but we aren't the people who make the decisions, Detective Oriscoe. We're the people who write down the decisions, then rewrite them in language that protects our clients from any parties who might think they are hurt by the deal."

"Ah. Fine. Has Brook protected any asset-strippers or corporate looters in the past six months?"

Myercough growled, but Merris held up his hand. "We'll check our records and provide you with a list of the deals that fell under Brook's umbrella. But remember, he's—forgive me—he *was* the senior partner. He had little to do with the terms of any deals his team worked on."

"Then what does a senior partner do?" asked Van Helsing.

Merris shrugged. "It's mainly managerial inside the firm. To our clients, we are the face of the firm. We take meetings, attend dinners or lunch meetings with clients, and address any concerns they might raise. Things like that."

"Then is there any possibility that Mr. Brook might have offended the wrong person?" asked Leery. "Say someone like Mama Rose Marie Van Dee? Someone with the pull to get a Barghest summoned and sent after him?"

Merris lifted one shoulder. "There's always the chance that Brook offended someone, but it's doubtful one of our clients would have the ability to dispatch a Barghest."

"Oh, come on, Counselor," said Leery. "You represent big money. Entrepreneurs. Monolithic corporations. Big deals like that always have a fixer on speed dial, right?"

"If they do, it is without our knowledge or participation," said Merris.

"Then it's possible."

"Detective, all things are possible in this universe."

"Huh," said Leery. "You've never seen me try to use Gaggle."

"Er...I'm afraid I don't understand."

"Gumball. Goofball." Leery pursed his lips for a moment, then snapped, smiling wide. "Gargle!"

"He means Google," said Dru with half a grin. "And he knows full well what the proper name is."

"Well...as I said, we will put together a list of clients for you."

"Right," said Leery. "Now, let's get down to the good stuff. What can you tell us about Richard Brook's social life?"

"Richard was single," said Myercough. "He dated, but..." The goblin shrugged.

"Did he date a lot? Anyone in particular?"

"He, uh, dated within his social sphere." Merris pursed his lips. "Richard was old money. They have their own hierarchies and social rules."

"And he stuck to them?" asked Dru.

"Yes, at least with women he'd see publicly," said Vastalan.

"And the ones he didn't see publicly?" asked Leery.

"In those cases he was concerned more with"—Merris glanced at Dru—"looks and body type."

"But if they were rich, he didn't care?"

"No, he still cared, but for his, uh, liaisons, he had a type."

"And what was that type?" asked Van Helsing.

"Pale-skinned, black hair."

"Could you be more specific? Sounds like my daughter," said Leery.

Merris made a vague gesture toward his face. "Done up. You know what I mean. Bright red lipstick, black eyeliner." He shrugged and blushed. "Richard, uh, liked *young* women."

"How young?" asked Epatha in a flat tone.

"Oh, nothing illegal," said Myercough. "But he liked his playthings new and shiny. Eighteen. Nineteen."

"And how old was Brook?" asked Leery.

Myercough sniffed. "He would have been ninety-seven this year."

Leery frowned. "The body we saw...he looked more like half that."

The goblin shrugged and flashed a malignant little grin. "Richard was an accomplished magus. He undertook certain practices..." The goblin peered at Van Helsing.

"Ah. All licensed?" said Dru. "And his young playthings?"

"Oh, he kept his paperwork up to date." Myercough grinned. "His...*friends*...may have lost some of their vigor for a time, but Richard never borrowed too much."

"How old are you two?" Leery asked, looking back and forth between the two magisters.

"I'm as old as I look," said Merris. "Forty-nine. I'm a simple wizard."

"And you?"

Myercough grinned. "My age is no concern of yours."

Leery pursed his lips.

SURE 'LOCK 21

"But I practice no rejuvenation spells. No essence manipulation."

"Any chance one of his society friends found out about his playthings?" asked Van Helsing. "Jealousy is a scranning cove and rarely stays cank for long."

"Uh…what?" asked Merris.

"To be sure, Lieutenant," said the goblin. "To be sure. But to answer your question, even if one of Richard's society conquests found out about the urchins he played with, they would not care. In those circles, a certain amount of *friskiness* is expected."

"I think we'll take a list of his society friends, all the same," she said.

"Of course," said Merris. "I'll see what I can put together. His housekeeper may know better."

"And her name?"

"Megan Moorehouse. She's almost as old as the house itself—and that was built in 1673." Merris smiled at Dru. "It's out in Brooklyn. A real beauty."

"I'm sure," said Dru.

"If he lived in Brooklyn, what was he doing in Hel's Kitchen?" asked Leery.

"He often stayed in his condo in the Sheffield building," said Merris. "He found the Midtown area more to his liking."

"No housekeeper there?"

"He had one, but she wouldn't be the one to speak to about the society girls."

"Ah. The Sheffield for the street urchins, and the old manse in Brooklyn for the society belles?"

"That's it," said Merris.

"We'll take her name either way," said Leery. "Never know where an investigation might lead."

Merris shrugged. "Maribel Izbia."

"And the Sheffield address?"

"The top floor, of course."

"Which unit?"

Myercough cackled. "The *whole* top floor, Detective."

"Right."

"Any other avenue we should stroll down?" asked Epatha.

"None that I can think of," said Merris. "Myer"—he coughed—"you ran in similar circles. Can you think of anything?"

"Let me disabuse you of the notion that Richard Brook's version of high society and mine had much in common. Humans and goblins don't mix." He heaved a sigh. "But I will think on it. I owe Richard that much."

"One last thing," Leery said. "Who benefits from Richard Brook's demise?"

"Financially, you mean?" asked Merris.

Leery shrugged.

"I'm sure he had a will. We *are* magisters. I'll see if I can find out who the executor is," said Myercough.

"But the immediate benefactors are Vastalan and me," said Harland Merris. "Our partnership agreement stipulates no shares are transferable outside the firm without a unanimous vote. Vast and I will probably inherit his shares equally."

"Meaning you just went from earning one-third of the firm's profits to one-half?"

Merris nodded. "Though the percentages aren't quite what you assume."

"Interesting," said Leery.

"We didn't have anything to do with his murder, though. Surely, you see that."

"Do I?"

"Of course!" snapped Myercough. "Don't be ridiculous, Detective. If we wanted to squeeze Richard out, we'd have done it a long time ago—and *lawfully*. He gave us plenty of opportunities."

"Like what?" asked Dru.

"His dalliances. We have a morality clause," said Myercough.

"Wait. Let me get this straight," said Leery. "A goblin would have used a morality clause to lawfully—"

"Is it so hard to believe?" demanded Myercough.

Leery glanced at Dru and tried not to grin. "Do you really want an answer to that question?"

4

Dru put the Crown Vic in gear, then glanced at Leery and put it back in park. She turned to face him better, studying his face. "You look tired."

"Nah. I just need to make a stop at Starbucks. A *trenta* will fix me up, right as rain."

"Chemicals won't stop you from passing out, Leery. Or from setting your rehabilitation back."

"I'm fine, Dru," he said in a soft voice. "I've reached the point where loafing around is doing more harm than good. Yes, I'll be exhausted at the end of the day—or maybe by lunch—but my mind *needs* this."

Dru cocked her head to the side and stared at him for a moment, then sketched five runes in a lovely green hue and connected them into a pentacle with lines of shimmering gold. She flicked it at him, and Leery shivered as the rune set settled on his skin. He closed his eyes a moment, then grinned. "You've been able to do that all this time and you never have? For shame, Dru Nogan! For shame!"

"Yeah, yeah. I can't—*won't*—do it again until after lunch. It could lead to trouble for your long-term health."

"Well, that's okay. I feel like I can go until dinner." He held up his index finger. "But we'll need that Starbucks stop either way."

"Of course we will," said Dru with a grin. She slid the car into drive and pulled away from the station house. "Where to first? Hel's Kitchen or Brooklyn?"

"I have a feeling the Brooklyn housekeeper will be harder to deal with, so let's go there first."

"Right. What's the address?"

"Exeter Street. You know, where the rich people live."

Dru shrugged and turned her attention to the traffic.

"But don't forget to—"

"—find us a Starbucks on the way," she finished for him with a grin.

"Hey, have you done this taking care of an injured partner thing before or what? You're plenty good at it."

Chapter 2
The Investigation

I

Dru pulled to the curb and put the cruiser in park. Creamy marble faced the house across the street and black wrought-iron pickets fenced it. Balconies faced the street on all three levels. Red brick pavers covered the small front yard. "This it?"

Leery peered at the address and nodded. "Yep. The Brook residence." He got out of the car and walked up to the front door. He pressed the doorbell, then glanced at Dru. "Nice parking job."

"Yeah," she said with a grin. Three of the cruiser's tires rested on the sidewalk. "I learned from the best."

"Oh, now I'll get the big head."

"I was referring to Gregory." She wrinkled her nose and stuck out her tongue.

"You're getting to enjoy that part, aren't you?"

The front door opened with a snap, and a matronly woman peered down her nose at them. "This block is designated no soliciting." Her voice was prim and icy cold.

"Bully for you," Leery said. "We're not selling anything."

"We're detectives," said Dru. "You are Ms. Megan Moorehouse?"

"Mrs. Moorehouse, if you please." She flicked her gaze back and forth between them. "I believe I'd like to see some identification."

"Sure," said Leery, flipping out his gold shield.

She peered at it, then gave them a single nod. "Mr. Brook is not at home, if he's who you are looking for—though I can't for the life of me imagine why you'd need to speak with him."

"May we come in?" asked Dru.

"As I said, Mr. Brook—"

"We're not here for him," said Leery. "We know where he is. We're here to speak to you, Mrs. Moorehouse."

"To me? Whatever for?"

"It would be better if we could speak inside."

Moorehouse shrugged, stepped back, and waved them inside. She led them to a sunken living room and sat on the edge of one of the upholstered chairs. "How may I help?"

"First, we've got some hard news," said Leery. "Mr. Brook was—"

"Mr. Brook perished this morning," said Dru.

Megan's eyes widened, and her lips made a perfect O before she covered them with a hand that shook. "How?" she asked, tears shimmering in her gray eyes.

"He was murdered," said Leery.

"I...I see." She closed her eyes and gave a minute shake of her head. "This is..."

"Unexpected," said Dru. "We understand."

"Then you want to know my whereabouts? What time—"

"No, Mrs. Moorehouse, you aren't a suspect," said Leery. "But we're hoping you can help us with a little information about Mr. Brook's social life."

"Social life? But I..." Megan shook her head.

"His partners said he often entertained ladies of society here," said Dru. "Parties and the like."

"Oh, yes," said Megan. "He was quite popular with women of a certain age. He is—*was* seen as an eligible bachelor, you see."

"We'd like a list of names," said Leery, digging out his leather-bound notepad.

"Names?"

"Of his girlfriends," said Leery, "or anyone who wanted to be one."

"It seems hardly proper for me to—"

"I'm afraid we must insist," said Dru.

"I see." She wiped wetness from her cheeks with the palms of her hands, showing no trace of self-consciousness. "He had a few admirers, but since he stopped spending time with Lena Cassidy, he hasn't had a steady interest."

"How long since they broke up?"

She treated Leery to a stern look. "Mr. Brook and Ms. Cassidy did not consort like common teenagers, sir. They did not *break up* but rather ended their association in a civil manner."

"Yeah, sure. Whatever. I only need to know when this civil-parting-of-the-ways took place."

Megan Moorehouse shrugged. "Two months ago?"

"Are you asking us or telling us?"

"Let me get his datebook and I'll tell you for sure." She stood and left them for a moment, and when she returned, she held a hard-bound ledger open across her palms. "Yes, here it is," she said. "Ms. Cassidy was last here nine weeks and three days ago."

"I see," said Dru. "And when was Mr. Brook's last visit to her home?"

Moorehouse nodded and scanned through the book. "He attended a soiree at her home seven weeks ago, but they had parted before that occasion."

"How can you be sure?"

Megan shrugged and snapped the ledger closed. "It occurred here."

"Any chance Ms. Cassidy may have been here, and the occasion didn't get recorded in the book?" asked Leery.

"None at all, sir." Megan sniffed. "How else may I help?"

"Got any coffee?"

"If you could give us Ms. Cassidy's contact information, we would be grateful," said Dru.

Megan's gaze danced back and forth between them for a moment, then she nodded once and disappeared.

"You don't have to ask everyone we talk to for coffee, Leery. You still have a full *trenta* in the car."

"Right, *in the car.*"

Dru shook her head but couldn't help but grin.

When Moorehouse returned, she held a slip of paper and a travel-cup of coffee.

2

Lena Cassidy lived a few streets away from Richard Brook's Manhattan Beach home. Her house was even bigger than his had been, and it straddled two lots by the look of it. A red Porsche 911 and a red Maserati Quattroporte GTS stood in the paved area between the front door and the street.

Dru turned the Crown Vic into the drive and pulled up behind the sports cars. She peered up at the curved front wall of the stone-wrapped house and pointed at the lights burning inside. "Looks like someone is home."

"Then let's go see if it's a murderer." They got out of the car and walked up to the massive double doors. Leery swung the brass knocker and stood back. "Not a bad way to live," he murmured, gesturing toward the south. "The beach is right there."

"I've never been," Dru said.

"Eh, one beach is like any other for the most part."

Dru shrugged. "I wouldn't know. I've never been to *any* beach."

"What?"

"There are none back home—no oceans—and I never got around to it up here."

"We'll have to—"

The door opened to reveal a man in a black suit. "Yes?"

"Is Ms. Lena Cassidy at home?" asked Leery.

"No," said the butler.

Leery hooked his thumb at the Porsche and the Maserati. "That's funny. The cars seem to be home."

The man sniffed. "She has many others. You may dial her social secretary and set an appointment."

"Ah," grunted Leery. "I already did that. Here's my invitation." He flipped out his golden NYPD detective's badge. "Detective Oriscoe is my name, and this is my partner, Detective Nogan. Where can we find Ms. Cassidy?"

"Let them in, Samson."

"Yes, ma'am." Samson stood back and invited them to enter with a wave. His face was carefully impassive.

"Thank you, Mr. Samson," said Dru as she patted him on the arm.

"Indeed, ma'am," he said. He turned and led them through a set of double doors into a fancy room filled with floral prints and pale pastels. "Ms. Cassidy, allow me to present Detectives Oriscoe and Nogan, from the New York Police Department's Supernatural Inquisitors Squad."

A tall, slender woman stood next to a glossy pink grand piano in a perfect beam of morning sunlight, her hand resting casually on the piano's lid. The sun twinkled on her jewelry—an elaborate necklace chock-a-block with fancy gems in blues, greens, opalescent white, and the shiny translucence of diamonds. Her lips bore a slight curve, but her eyes did little to add warmth to the chilly room.

"Ms. Cassidy? I'm Leery Oriscoe and this is—"

"Drusilla bat Agrat," finished Lena Cassidy. "I'm a devotee of your aunt."

"Ah," said Dru. "Lilith? Naamah?"

Lena's smile grew a touch colder. "No. Eisheth Zenunim. The one your aunts and mother shun."

"Well, Auntie Naamah and Auntie Eisheth don't get along, and Aunt Lily goes along with Auntie Naamah, but as far as shunning anyone, that's not the case at all. Mother's caught in the middle. She and Auntie Eisheth visit one another often."

Lena gave a bland smile. "Thank you for correcting me."

Dru cocked her head and raised her eyebrows for a moment before turning her head to survey the room. "I take it you are a maleficent in Eisheth's tradition?"

Lena lifted her chin. "I'm the Grand Mater of the Brooklyn Coven."

"Ah, I was wondering about that," said Leery. "You got any coffee around this joint?"

Lena narrowed her eyes at Dru's profile. "Is that a problem?"

Dru turned a bored gaze on Cassidy. "Hardly," she said. "I understand you used to spend time with Richard Brook?"

Lena nodded. "What of it? We parted ways some weeks back."

"Yes," said Leery. "Megan Moorehouse told us... Say, about that coffee—"

"And how is dear Megan?" asked Lena.

"She seemed fine," said Leery. "She's very generous with *her* coffee."

Cassidy snapped a quick glance in his direction. "Coffee? What is all this about coffee?"

"Ignore him, sister," said Dru. "He's a lunatic."

Lena turned back to Dru. "What's this about...*sister*?"

"It's about your ex-boyfriend," said Leery. "Richard Brook."

Cassidy sighed. "And what about him?"

"Well, he's dead for one thing," said Dru in a cold voice.

Lena Cassidy's eyes widened, but her face remained cold and hard as though chiseled from fine marble. "Oh," she said.

"Yeah, your ex was murdered this morning," said Leery. "By someone skilled in summoning." He pivoted on his heel and gazed at Dru. "Hey, Dru, about this *Maleficium* Whatsit your Auntie runs—"

"*Maleficium Zenunim!*" snapped Lena.

A soft grin brightened Dru's face. "It's sex magic, Leery. No summoning involved."

"What, like a succubus?" Leery's gaze bounced from Dru to Lena and back. "Like..."

"No, not like a succubus," said Dru. "Like a witch who *wants to be* a succubus."

"Ah," said Leery in a tone that made his continued confusion clear. "Like... Well..."

"Unlike your partner, Detective, I can't get by on pheromones and sultry looks. I have to work for my supper."

"Oh... So, you still..."

Lena smiled a wicked smile. "Yes. I still consume the souls of my mates."

Leery shook his head. "Where's the fun in that?"

"Lena uses magic to seduce, then more magic to drain her target's soul energy to bolster her own life."

"Oh." Leery shook his head. "I guess you've got a ticket for that?"

"But of course," said Lena. She glanced at Samson, and the butler turned and left the room. "I keep it in the safe upstairs. There's no telling what a ticket is worth to someone without the breeding and status to get one."

"Uh...right," said Leery. "Your designated prey belongs to what class?"

Lena's smile twitched. "Males who are interested in supernatural augmentation of pleasure. I prefer them young—for obvious reasons—but virile goes a long way, too." She ran a lascivious hand down her side.

"No, dear," said Dru with a strident note in her voice. "You'd do well to check who marks him before you endanger your life."

Lena narrowed her eyes and looked Leery up and down. Her eyes widened, and she put her fingers to her lips. "I meant nothing by it," she murmured.

"Besides," said Leery with a shaky smile, "I'm old enough to be your father."

"No, you're not," said Lena with a secret smile.

"Let's, uh, talk about Mr. Brook. I take it you know about his…hobbies?"

Lena chuckled. "You mean that Richie liked to dabble with the emo crowd?" She shrugged. "When I first became aware of what he was doing in the Sheffield, I mentioned a thing or two about *Maleficium Zenunim* practices—strictly out of curiosity, mind you—but most of it he already knew."

"Knew how?" asked Dru.

"He was a most knowledgeable magus, you know. He had a penchant for rare magical texts."

"Ah," said Leery. "Did he belong to any organized practice?"

"Once, I'm sure, but not for decades."

"And which one did he participate in back in the day?"

"He was a member of the *Sigillum Sanctum Fraternitatis*. He attained the rank of Magus—in the Order of the Silver Star."

"Ah," said Dru. "The *Arcanum Arcanorum*."

"Indeed," said Lena. "You know it?"

"Of course. Aleister is a longtime friend of the family."

"Of course, he is," said Lena with a smile. "Richard was a contemporary of dear Aleister."

Dru nodded. "Then perhaps we should speak to him."

Lena wagged her head to the side. "He may know something I don't—especially about Richard's history. I've only known him a few decades." Her expression froze. "I only knew him that long, I mean."

"I think that's the first reaction to the news I've seen from you," said Leery.

The witch shrugged. "We all react in diverse ways, Detective." She caressed the piano's top.

"Ah."

"Thank you for seeing us," said Dru.

"Anytime, Your Grace," said Cassidy with a slight bow.

"We'll show ourselves out."

They retraced their steps to their cruiser, and Dru got Leery situated in the passenger seat, even doing up his seatbelt, then circled around to sit behind the wheel. "Let me call Uncle Aleister's office for an appointment."

"We could just go over to the courthouse. We're close."

Dru shook her head. "No, it's better to set an appointment. He'd feel pressured to see me if I drop by—even if he's on the bench—and I don't want that."

"Fine," said Leery. "Maybe there's a Starbucks around."

"After I set the appointment, we can go to the Sheffield and talk to Maribel Izbia. I wonder what surprises she has in store for us."

"What, no coffee?"

"You have to pace yourself, Leery. You haven't had this much coffee since the Agon case, and you're not up to form. I don't want you freaking out on me." She started the car before turning her teasing grin on him.

He returned a one-sided smile. "Very funny. You scared me for a minute. I thought you were turning into a prude."

"A prudish succubus?" Dru arched an eyebrow at him as she dropped the Ford into reverse. "I'm not sure how that would work."

"Well, first it starts with a misunderstanding of coffee, then—"

"Yeah, yeah."

3

Dru shouldered her way through the door of the Starbucks a block from the Sheffield. She carried a tray of giant *trenta*-sized cups and a brown paper bag emblazoned with the logo of the chain. Leery rolled down the window as she approached his door and reached for one of the cups, but Dru pulled the tray out of reach. "No," she said. "Take the bag."

"What's this? Did Starbucks invent a way to keep coffee in a brown paper sack? That's genius!"

"Take the bag, Lerome," said Dru in her best I'm-gonna-kick-your-wolf-ass growl. "Eat a bit of what you find inside, and *then* you can have more coffee."

"Uh...*eat*?"

"Yes, dork. Eat."

Leery made a face and reached for the bag with two fingers but pulled his hand back before he touched it. "You know Starbucks is a *coffee shop*, right?"

"How could I not?" Dru said, arching her eyebrow. "But you're still recovering, and you *will* eat this. It's that, or I call Uncle Luci and he'll revoke your work status."

"Hey, Dru, that's not—"

"Yes, it is. It was one of his conditions. You are to eat something every two to three hours, or every two gallons of coffee."

"Yeah, I can understand the time thing, but I can drink two gallons of coffee in—"

"It's not a negotiation, Leery," said Dru. "Now, take the bag and eat."

Leery sighed and reached for the bag once more, hooking it with one finger, his lips curled. "Have you ever eaten coffee-shop food, Dru?"

"Lerome Oriscoe, you eat sandwiches out of vending machines!"

He puffed out his cheeks and looked in the bag. "Oh, thank the Whole Bean, I thought it would be a salad!" He sniffed a long breath. "Chicken and bacon! Excellent choice." He pulled half the sandwich out of the bag and wolfed it down. "Oh, my! That's delicious!" He withdrew the other half and it disappeared in a few giant bites. "I was wrong, Dru! I *was wrong*!"

"Apology accepted," she said with a grin. "There's another one in the bag."

"Yeah, I'm saving it for later. I've got to pace myself. I've been under-the-weather, you know."

With a roll of her eyes, Dru handed over the coffee, and Leery secured the extra coffees in the custom cup-holder Bryant Wheelbarrowx and Regina Deal had sent him as a get-well present. She got in and pulled the car around the block, then up onto the sidewalk in front of the Sheffield, ignoring the doorman's comical expression. She came around as Leery hopped out.

"That really hit the spot, Dru," he said. "Nothing wrong with a little sandwich to wash down the coffee once in a while."

She grinned. "I think it's the other way around."

"Nah. Not unless you're a sissy." He turned and walked into the building, tapping his gold shield and grinning at the doorman. He strode through the lobby and into the elevator as if he owned the place. He pressed the button for the penthouse, then grimaced when the button didn't light up.

Dru tapped the keyhole next to the button and beckoned the doorman. "Penthouse, please," she called.

The doorman shifted his gaze between them and the Crown Vic sitting askew on the sidewalk, then shook his head and came on the run, sorting through keys on his chained keyring. "Are you going to leave it there?" he mumbled.

"Sure. Cops—we park where we want," said Leery.

"And we won't be long," said Dru. "We have an appointment Downtown in forty minutes."

"Uh..." The doorman turned his key in the elevator panel and pressed the penthouse button, then looked at the cruiser again. "What do I say if someone wants to leave a ticket?"

"You tell them Leery Oriscoe said to leave it the fu—"

"Tell them we're on official business." Dru fished out her card and handed it over. "And then hang onto the card in case you ever need a favor."

The doorman smiled and slipped the card into the side pocket of his jacket. "Yes, Ma'am," he said. The elevator doors closed on his beaming smile.

"Well, that's one way," said Leery.

"Sometimes, Leery, honey is better than vinegar."

"And sometimes coffee is better than either of those."

"Coffee, again?"

"Yeah. I mean, have you ever tried *drinking* vinegar? And don't get me started on honey. The slow, gloopy drink." He hooked his fingers in the air as if anyone in the world had ever called honey 'the slow, gloopy drink,' and he was quoting them.

"You know what you are, Oriscoe? Nuts," she said.

"No, Dru, that's where you're wrong. Coffee comes from *beans*."

The elevator doors slid open, saving her from having to reply. The Sheffield's penthouse was huge, with stunning views of the park, Midtown, Hel's Kitchen, and the Hudson in the distance.

"Who's there?"

"Police," said Leery. "Detectives Nogan and Oriscoe."

A petite woman with half a head of green hair and half a head of jet-black hair came out of a hall that led to the back of the flat. Her

SURE 'LOCK   49

lipstick was bright, bright scarlet—so bright it made her lips look like neon tubes against her alabaster skin. "I didn't do it," she said with a smile.

"Are you Maribel Ibzia?" asked Dru.

"Yes, Detective Oriscoe."

"I'm Nogan, he's Oriscoe."

She glanced at Leery and grinned, exposing her dainty fangs. "Well, you said—"

"Yeah, this is what I get for being polite and putting her first."

Maribel dimpled. "If you're here for Mr. Brook—"

"You haven't heard then?" asked Leery. "I wouldn't have guessed that goblin would be so tight-lipped."

"Heard what?" Her expression shifted from amused to wary in a heartbeat. "Has something happened to Rich?"

"Rich, is it?" asked Dru. "That's a heavy dose of familiarity for a—"

"Rich doesn't care about convention, formality. Plus, I've known him a long time. Nearly three years."

"My, that *is* a long time," said Leery in a droll tone.

"What's happened?" Maribel wailed, lips quivering.

"Mr. Brook was killed this morning," said Dru.

The dainty housekeeper threw her arm over her eyes and swooned as melodramatically as any Vaudeville actress ever had. Leery rushed forward and caught her before she hit the ground, then glanced at Dru. "She's out."

Dru arched her eyebrows. "Quick, I'll go through her purse while you put her on the couch."

Leery frowned down at the housekeeper, but Maribel didn't so much as twitch. "No, I think she's really fainted."

Dru shrugged. "Give her to me. I'll put her on the couch."

"It's no big deal. She weighs about as much as Van Helsing." He bent and hooked an arm behind her knees, then straightened with a grunt.

"See? You should've listened to me."

"That's going to be on my tombstone, I think," he mumbled.

"It is if I outlive you," said Dru with a cocky smile. "Now, give her to me and go sit down before you faint."

"No, I'm fine." He took a step toward the couch, then stopped and closed his eyes. "Can you come get her?"

With an eye roll, Dru took Maribel and laid her on the couch. She patted one pale cheek, then the other. "Come on, Maribel. Wakey-wakey."

Leery slouched into an overstuffed La-Z-Boy and took a deep breath. "This... Uh. Hey, remember when we...you...did that thing on the way to Brooklyn?"

"The rune set of invigoration?"

"Yeah, green with golden lines?"

"I said not until after lunch."

"Hey, I ate, didn't I?"

Dru shook her head. "Not until after noon, Leery." Her face settled into solemn lines as she returned his gaze. "Too much could be bad news."

"Yeah, okay," he said, letting his eyelids sink closed. "I'll rest while she—"

"Wha..." Maribel thrashed her head from side to side. "No. No."

"Wake up, Ms. Ibzia," said Dru.

"Well, I'm refreshed," said Leery, blowing his cheeks out.

"No," said the housekeeper. "If I'm awake and you two are here that means Rich..." She squeezed her eyelids tighter.

"Look, Maribel, you can waste time denying the truth, or you can help us find out who killed him."

The diminutive woman's eyes flew open and she sat up. "Someone *killed* him?"

"Early this morning," said Dru.

"Or something," said Leery. "Maybe a Barghest."

"A... What?"

"You know," said Leery, jerking his head toward Dru. "An evil dog-like thing."

"What? That makes no sense." Maribel sat up, patting at her hair. "A Barghest is an *omen* of death, not a deliverer of it."

"This particular hound bit Mr. Brook to death," said Dru.

Maribel's face drew down into a grimace of confusion, and she toyed with her bottom lip but didn't smear the crimson on her lips.

"You fed recently," said Dru.

"What? Oh, yes." She flapped her hand. "Rich and I shared a meal just last night."

"How's that work?" asked Leery. "I thought the magus needed lifeforce to do his little trick."

"Yeah," said Maribel. "I only need the blood."

"I suppose your license is in order?" asked Dru.

"Yes. Rich keeps all that up to date for me," she said with a bright smile. "It pays to have friends in high…" Her face crumpled, and tears of blood smeared in her eyes.

"Uh, let's talk about this meal," said Leery. "What was her name?"

"Was? I don't kill when I feed, Detective. Neither did Rich. She'll be fine in a few days."

"Her name?" asked Dru.

"Jathy…" Her gaze wandered to Leery's. "Uh… What did you say your name was?"

"Jathy *Oriscoe*?" he said, leaning toward her.

She winced. "Um…yeah. Are you… *Are you her dad*?"

Leery shot out of the chair and lunged across the space dividing them. "What did you do to her?"

"Nothing she didn't want!" squeaked Maribel.

"Where is she?" His voice had spiraled down to a rough growl, and his eyes sparkled with anger.

"She's fine, I swear! Rich had her driven home after—" Her eyes widened, and her voice cut off with another squeak.

"Call her, Leery," said Dru.

Leery fished out his phone, then shook his head and shoved it back into his pocket. "You do it. She won't pick up for me. 555-6875"

Dru rose with a nod and got out her phone, then walked a short distance. She dialed and held the phone to her ear.

Leery watched her for a moment longer then turned back to glower at Ibzia. "If she's hurt…"

"I swear, Detective Oriscoe, she's not! I'm…I'm…*small*. I-I-I don't take much."

"And *Rich*?" he sneered.

"He never took much from anyone. He has a constant supply. He never needs to do lasting damage to—"

"*Lasting* damage?"

Maribel pulled her legs up and wrapped her arms around them. "She'll be fine in a day or two. Until then she'll—"

SURE 'LOCK   55

Leery took another step closer and bent down to put his face in hers. "And did you *make* her for her trouble?" he snarled.

"Leery!" called Dru, holding out her phone. "Come talk to your daughter."

With one last glowering snarl, Leery hurried over and took the phone from Dru. "Jathy? Jathy, honey? Are you okay?"

Dru walked over to the couch. "She'd better be okay," she said. "Do you know who Hercule DuSang is?"

Maribel nodded, but she kept sneaking looks at Leery.

"Good. I'm his daughter," said Dru.

The small vampire's head snapped back to stare at Dru, and her eyes grew very wide.

"If his daughter bears any lasting marks…" Dru raised her hands out to her sides and smiled down at Maribel sweetly. "I'll stake you myself," she hissed.

Maribel twitched back on the couch, putting as much space as she could muster between them. "I already said we never took so much as to cause lasting damage."

"Sure, because feeding vampires and liches are such good judges of when enough is enough."

Ibzia dropped her gaze toward the floor. "Did *he* do it?"

"Do what?"

"Kill Rich?"

"Don't be absurd!" snapped Dru. "He's a cop for one thing, and he just found out you fed on his daughter a few seconds ago. What, do you think he can time travel?"

"Can he?" Maribel asked as her gaze snapped up and her eyes widened.

Dru scoffed. "You'd better start that pin cushion you call a brain. You'd better start thinking about who might have had it out for Brook. Which of his victims might—"

"Victims? *Victims!* It wasn't like that. They were all willing participants. They-they signed papers for Rich acknowledging that."

"Where are these papers?" Dru backed away from the couch and held up a hand. "Take me to them." She glanced at Leery, who stood stock-still, his shoulders hunched, the phone pressed to his ear, then her gaze snapped back to Maribel. "Up! Take me to these papers!"

The vampire unfolded slowly, extending her leg as if to test the surface before putting her weight on it. "I'm sure they're in his office, but he has a safe."

SURE 'LOCK 57

"Show me."

Maribel stood and led her to the back of the apartment, down a long hall past numerous lavishly decorated bedrooms, and into a wood-paneled room the size of a small apartment. A massive oak desk stood across a thick Persian carpet. A matching oak cabinet stood in the corner behind the desk, and she pointed at it. "The safe's in there." She crossed to a set of oak filing cabinets decorated with bas-relief of courtroom scenes. "But they might also be in here." She glanced at the row of cabinets. "Somewhere."

"Well, then you'd better get started looking. What's the combination to the safe?"

"I..." The housekeeper hung her head. "I don't know."

"Maribel, don't give me reason to doubt your cooperation."

"He said I had no reason to know it."

Dru scoffed and walked to the cabinet, opening the double doors on its front. The safe was a forged-steel behemoth with biometric input. "Most of these biometric deals also have a hidden keyhole in case of emergency." She looked over her shoulder at Maribel. "Where would Brook have put the key?"

"Hmm. Maybe the bottom right desk drawer. There's a metal file box in there where he kept some things."

Dru walked to the desk and opened the drawer. Inside was a metal box with a key lock lid that covered the contents of the drawer. "And the key to this?"

"Probably not locked," said Maribel without looking up from the file folder she'd pulled out.

"Something?"

"What? Oh." The housekeeper's cheeks turned a little pink—a high blush for a pale-skinned vampire. "My, uh, employment file." She closed it and slid it on top of the cabinet. "I'll go through it later."

"No, you won't," said Dru as she crossed the room. She snatched the file folder and carried it back to the desk. "This is evidence. The paperwork is the only thing I've authorized you to find." She sat in Brook's chair and tried the lid in the bottom drawer. It opened, revealing a hodgepodge of loose items—including a glass jar of small keys. "Great," she muttered.

"Here they are!" said Maribel with an air of relief. She turned toward Dru and held out a thick manilla folder.

"Good," said Dru. "Now, you need to leave."

"What? Why?"

"You can't stay here while we investigate this as a possible crime scene."

"But...I *live* here."

"Not anymore," said Dru. "The owner of this property was murdered, Maribel. And he was here until shortly before the murder occurred. This apartment may contain evidence—"

"Where do I go?"

Dru shrugged. "Rent your own apartment, book a hotel."

"I don't have much money," whined Maribel. "Rich said this would always be my home."

"Find an empty grave or stay with a friend, then! We need to process the apartment." She waved her hands to encompass Brook's apartment. "The crime scene team will be here soon, and the apartment will be sealed to non-police personnel until their investigation is finished. After that, I imagine it will be released to the executor of Richard Brook's will or, if we can't find him today, Harland Merris or Vastalan Myer—" she coughed.

"That goblin," sneered Maribel. "He's a ratty bastard. Richard didn't trust him. Said he was a greedy asshole."

Dru arched an eyebrow. "Is that so?"

"Yes." Maribel crossed her arms over her chest. "Where am I supposed to go?"

"Wherever you decide, I'd suggest you do it before Detective Oriscoe gets off the phone with his daughter. He's a werewolf, you know."

Ibzia paled, and her hand fluttered up to cover her mouth. Then, she turned and darted from the room, running halfway down the hall and dipping into one of the bedrooms.

Dru's face warped with a vicious little smile her mother would have approved of.

4

Dru returned to the living room after Maribel huffed out of the apartment carrying two huge suitcases. Leery sat in one of the La-Z-Boys, looking hangdog, Dru's phone held loosely in one hand. He'd loosened his tie and unbuttoned the top of his thick poplin dress shirt.

"Is she okay?" Dru asked.

Leery flopped his hand. "I guess. She said no one forced her. That it was none of my business anyway. That I shouldn't get in the way of her dreams."

"Want me to talk to her?"

"A lot of good it will do. She thinks I'm a hypocrite, being a wolf and denying her right to convert to a supernatural."

Dru moved over to the chair and stood at his side. "I could explain your feelings about the conversion process. I could—"

"It's okay, Dru," said Leery with a sigh. "This isn't the cause of our separation. It's the latest in a long line of things."

"But I don't mind, Leery. And I could introduce her to the right kind of vampires. Old ones with a sense of honor. Vampires who might be able to remove the romantic veneer of being undead."

"Maybe," he said. "I appreciate the offer, no matter what we end up doing."

Dru nodded. "Hinton is on her way with a team to process the place." She stood and took her phone gently. "He had all of his...meals...sign a release and a statement of free will. He was legal."

Leery grimaced. "I don't want—"

Dru smiled and handed him the forms Jathy had signed. "Officially, Jathy was never here."

Leery turned his face to look up at her. "Thank you."

She smiled and nodded. "Come on, we're going to be late for our chat with Uncle Aleister."

5

Leery didn't say much as Dru navigated the traffic and parked behind the courthouse. He did, however, manage to finish off one of his *trentas* and half of the other sandwich. By the time they got out, his pallor had mostly gone away, and his smile appeared as she held out a hand to help him out of the car.

Aleister Crowley met them at the door to his chambers, a cheery smile on his face. "Your Grace!" He bowed over her hand and pressed his insubstantial lips to it. "I'm so happy to see you. How is your delightful royal mother? And His Majesty, your uncle, of course."

"Hello, Uncle Aleister," she said with a dimple or two. "You're looking well! Mother and Uncle Luci are fine, as always."

"I'd, uh, heard about Her Majesty's recent visit to Manhattan." His eyes cut to Leery. "So glad to see you up and about, Detective."

"You and me, both, Your Honor," said Leery. "Getting back to work has been a great thing, even though I know I'm going to be in a coma tonight."

"Oh! Where are my manners?" Crowley flickered like a strobe at a rave. "Come in! Come in and sit!"

Dru and Leery walked into the room, and Crowley frowned at the door handle, then reached for it. His flickering hand passed through it, and he stole a glance at Dru, then tried again. "Bloody thing!" he muttered. He switched his fierce attention to the door itself and managed to give it a shove, then watched it swing slowly closed. "There!" He turned and beamed a smile at them, then floated over to his desk and leaned against it, facing them. "How I love a good visit!"

Dru smiled up at him for a moment, then said, "Uncle Aleister, I'm afraid this is not just a social call. We're on a case, and we think the victim is an old friend of yours."

Aleister Crowley frowned but nodded. "Yes. Poor Richard. His partner, that goblin, came by earlier this morning to gloat."

"Ah," said Leery. "Myer"—he coughed—"sure seems to have made the rounds."

"Yes," said Crowley with a slight frown. "He's a distasteful one but not a lazy one."

"Uncle Aleister, I need to ask you about the *Arcanum Arcanorum*," said Dru.

Crowley grimaced and folded his arms across his chest. "I left all that behind, Your Grace."

"We know, but isn't it true you and Richard were close? That Richard was a Magus in the Order of the Silver Star?"

"Oh, yes," said Aleister. "He was quite ambitious to learn the magical arts." He smiled bitterly. "You could say he was driven, and that he let nothing stand in his way."

"You mean friendship, family?" asked Leery.

"Indeed. He aggressively pursued any hint of magic, any grimoire, any therimoire, or scrap of an incantation. He lusted for dominion and spells that exalted his power."

"Like essence manipulation?" asked Dru.

Aleister's frown deepened. "Indeed, and such practices..." He shook his head and slid a little deeper into his desk's top. "It drove a wedge through the *Sigillum Sanctum Fraternitatis*. Jealousy, mostly, but also the understandable reaction to Richard's hubris."

"Anyone in particular?" asked Leery.

Crowley met his gaze and flashed a grim smile. "Me, for one. His attitude and experiments became a millstone around my neck. We parted ways over it and haven't spoken since. I ignored him."

"Any others? Anyone who didn't take the path you settled on?"

"Many others, Detective." He pursed his lips. "But perhaps one more so than the others. Bevin Gemble-Croix."

"And what did Gemble-Croix do that stood out?"

Aleister sighed. "It was a different time. We had only vague knowledge of the Nine Realms, of personages like Her Grace. We often did things we only half-believed in. Gemble-Croix was just arrogant enough not to care if his actions had real repercussions or not."

"Okay," said Leery with a shrug.

"Bevin cursed Richard Brook and his lineage. What we considered a powerful curse." He glanced at Dru, then ducked his gaze. "One that invoked certain entities in Gehenna."

"A Barghest," said Dru with a nod.

"Yes. Bevin's curse supposedly attached one of the creatures to Richard's lifeforce, tasking it to watch him and any of his offspring, tallying their evil-doings and whisking them to the afterlife once a certain threshold was met."

A line appeared between Dru's eyebrows.

"As I said, Your Grace, we had a limited understanding of what we were doing. We certainly had not yet pierced the veil to Gehenna ourselves."

"But a curse like you describe..."

Aleister nodded. "Yes. And once we made contact and were brought into the Covenancy proper, we all thought the curse was nonsense, but now..." He raised his hands and shrugged.

"Is Gemble-Croix still, uh..."

"Alive?" asked Aleister with a smile. "Yes, Detective, he's alive and still practicing magic. But he must be a centenarian by now. I'd imagine he's quite frail." His smile slowly transformed into a frown. "Unless he followed in Richard's footsteps."

"You haven't maintained contact?" asked Leery.

Crowley shook his head. "No, I found him distasteful after his so-called curse. I blackballed him from the *Arcanum Arcanorum* and stripped him of his rank."

"But that didn't stop him?"

"No. I believe he joined with the Temple of Mot."

"Uncle Aleister, did you ever speak with my mother or uncle about this curse?"

"No, Your Grace. I was…embarrassed."

She nodded once and glanced at Leery.

"You're not saying there might be something to this?" Leery asked.

Aleister grimaced. "She is, Detective. The Barghest are creatures apart. Wild creatures, if you will, but semi-intelligent. They can be bound as with other de…lesser entities of Gehenna if one has the will and the proper spells."

A silence fell between them for a few moments, then Dru put a warm smile on her lips and stood. "Thank you, Uncle Aleister. This helps."

"Uh, right," said Leery. "Do you know where this Gemble-Croix has spent the intervening years?"

Aleister shook his head. "Indeed, I don't, but I can endeavor to find out."

"That would be great," said Dru, flashing her dimples again. "But we'd better get back to it. If there's a Barghest running around Manhattan, we'd better get it caged in a hurry."

"Must you go so soon?" asked Crowley.

"I'm afraid so, Uncle Aleister," said Dru. "Perhaps, if we can wrap this case up by then, we could get together over the weekend?"

"I'd love to," said Aleister. "Let me know where and when, and I'll be there."

They left Crowley's chambers and found an elevator waiting. Leery leaned against the wall of the car, even though they only had to ride it down two floors. His haggard face tended toward pale again, and his eyelids drooped. "What now? Find the local Temple of Mot and ask about this Gemble-Croix character?"

Dru gave him an assessing look. "No, now we go to lunch, and maybe you have a little nap."

"Nah. I'm okay."

"Maybe," said Dru. "But I'm still the boss of you, tomato-face, and what I say goes."

Even his grin looked weak and disappeared too soon. "Lunch sounds good."

"Damn right, and you'll eat every bite."

6

Dru wrote pleasant green runes in the air between them, then connected the runes with shimmering golden lines. She lay the rune set across his chest and smiled at his sudden intake of breath. "There, you big baby," she said.

"Whew! Thanks, Dru. Lunch, plus that spell, and I feel like I could hop a marathon."

"Don't you mean 'run?'"

"No, I mean 'hop.' Like a bunny."

"Okaaay…"

"Hey, it's easy to run. *Anyone* can run and look cool. Try hopping like a bunny and pulling off cool."

"At least I know you're really feeling better," murmured Dru as she started the car.

"So, where are we headed? Temple of Mot?"

"No. I called Hinton while you were powdering your nose"—Dru wrinkled her nose—"and she's already got this Gemble-Croix's address."

"Oh. That was fast."

"Yep. But he was easy for her to find."

"Yeah? Why's that?"

Dru grinned. "She said you'd ask that and gave me an answer."

"Oh, goody. I can't wait."

"She said, and I quote, 'I'm just that good, Laika.'"

Leery grunted.

"Admit it, Oriscoe. You missed being called by a famous dog's name."

He shrugged. "Maybe a little. By *Hinton*."

Dru chuckled and put the car in gear. "You'll never guess where Gemble-Croix lives."

"Give me a hint, and maybe I will."

"It's between Lexington and Park."

He looked at her and frowned. "No."

"Yes. Right across the street from our old friend, Antoine LaSalle."

Leery grimaced. "I'd like to run into that old vamp again."

"Maybe not today, though, okay?" Dru said.

"Yeah. Maybe not."

Dru took Park Avenue and turned east on 70th Street. She pulled up in front of a swanky building, just west of where they'd fought and captured Antoine LaSalle, *de facto* leader of the Dead Set. His building looked decrepit, abandoned, but then again, it hadn't looked like much before LaSalle faded from public view.

Leery sighed. "At least he had to become even more of a hermit than before. That's almost like serving time, right?"

Dru glanced at the building and gave him a single nod. "We're not here for LaSalle, Leery."

"No," he agreed, turning his head to look at the fancy place across the street. It rose five stories above the street level, including the mansard roof. The second and third-floor rooms facing the street bore graceful bay windows with copper surrounds that had oxidized to a lovely green. "Come on. We're off to see the wizard."

"Warlock, Leery. Gemble-Croix is a warlock."

"We need to get you caught up on your reading, my dear," Leery said with a grin as he opened his door. "Or maybe your classic movies."

Dru grinned. "I know the *Wizard of Oz*, silly. I was pulling your leash." She winked at him and popped out of the car.

He looked at the car a moment and tsked. "Only one tire on the curb? You're slipping, partner."

"Yeah, yeah. Get over there and ring the bell before I ring yours."

Leery wagged his eyebrows. "All talk, no action makes Dru a chaste woman."

Her cheeks turned pink, and she dropped her gaze. She crossed the street ahead of him and pressed the doorbell. Leery joined her as the door opened with a creak.

"Yes," said an ancient butler dressed in black tails.

"We'd like to see Bevin Gemble-Croix," said Dru.

"Have you an appointment?"

"No," said Leery, "but we're—"

"I'm afraid the master doesn't admit common urchins from the street."

With a one-sided grin, Leery flipped out his shield and tapped it. "He'll see us, or we'll come back with a search warrant."

The butler sniffed. "One moment." He closed the door in their faces.

"Well, at least we know he's still an arrogant bastard," said Leery. After fifteen minutes of waiting, he pressed the doorbell and held it down for a few moments.

The butler snatched the door open and glared out at them. "One must have time to move back and forth between the master's chambers and the door!"

"Yeah, yeah," grumbled Leery. "Now, which way did the *master* want it? Search warrant or—"

"The master wishes you to do your worst." The butler began to swing the door closed, but Dru pushed it open.

"Tell him Drusilla bat Agrat bat Mahlat stands on his threshold and is growing angry." The timbre of her voice roughened, deepened, like faraway thunder, and the butler paled.

"O-one moment, Your G-grace," he stammered. He moved the door a fraction of an inch, then met her gaze and fell back a few steps. "Or-or-or...yuh-you could tell him."

Dru nodded and swept past him with a regal flick of her hair. "Come along, Leery," she called over her shoulder.

With a wide grin, Leery followed her into the house. The building seemed to contain a single household. British Colonial furnishings and interior design dominated what they could see of it. Dru paused at the other end of the wood-floored foyer and half-turned back to flick her gaze at the butler. "Where is he?" she asked in a tone at home in an arctic gale.

"Third floor. Take the stairs, then right around the landing to the room closest to the street."

Dru sniffed and climbed the majestic staircase with Leery huffing and puffing behind her. "Are you okay?" she whispered.

"Go on ahead," he wheezed. "But save the best snark for when I get there." He grinned up at her and shooed her on, but she turned and came back down to where he leaned against the banister and snaked her arm through his.

"Lean on me a little."

"No, really, it's—"

"Don't make me pull rank on you, Oriscoe."

A wan grin washed across his face. "Dru, *I'm* the detective sergeant. That means I outrank you by…a lot."

"But that's not what matters, Leery," she said with sweet a grin. "I'm a *princess*."

"Well, you've got me there."

"Damn right, I do. Now, shut up and give me some of your weight."

They continued up the stairs at a slower pace—one Dru made seem regal and proud rather than exhausted and washed-out. On the third floor, where the majestic staircase ended, they rested a moment on an upholstered bench that seemed more decorative than useful but served Leery's purposes just the same.

The room closest to the street took up half of the third floor, an elaborate mahogany door and casing set in the middle of the wall. Dru approached the door and flung it open, glaring into an afternoon-sun-warmed room. Bookcases lined the walls, and a desk sat opposite the bed, stacked high with parchment scrolls and old books.

A creature made of loose skin and wispy, brittle white hair squawked from a huge bed situated to get most of the light. "Who are you? Why are you troubling my door? Who let you in? Frederick! Frederick! What have you done to my butler? Frederick!" He gathered the stained front of his long once-white old-fashioned sleeping gown and covered his face.

Dru gathered a deep breath, then boomed, "I am Drusilla bat Agrat bat Mahlat, Princess of Gehenna, and *how dare you* leave me waiting on your stoop like a common servant!"

The man on the bed whimpered and tried to swim to the other side of the bed.

"Oh, you're in trouble," Leery taunted.

"I... I..."

"Bevin Gemble-Croix?" Dru thundered.

"Yuh-yes."

"Glad to meet you," she said in her normal voice. "How nice of you to make time to see us. May we sit?"

"Um... Where is Frederick?" His rheumy gaze darted back and forth between Dru and Leery. "Why isn't he here to announce you?"

Leery chuckled. "He didn't like the idea of being caught between Her Grace's wrath and your own. I think he's hiding downstairs."

Dru strolled into the room, found a stuffed armchair, and brought it over to the bed for Leery before going back for another for herself. She sat between Gemble-Croix and the window, crossed her legs, crossed her forearms over her knees, and leaned toward him. "There's a matter we need to discuss, Gemble-Croix."

"A-a-a matter?"

Leery leaned back in the chair. "Say, do you like coffee, Bevin?"

"What? Coffee? Barbaric drink! I prefer Darjeeling with honey and just a touch of milk."

"Savage," grunted Leery.

"You invoked a denizen of Gehenna in a curse, Gemble-Croix." Dru's tone was lackadaisical, mild.

"What? A curse? I've hurled no curse!"

"Does the name Richard Brook mean anything to you?" asked Leery.

"Richard..." The old man's face paled. "But that was..."

"I need to see the exact wording of the spell," said Dru. "I need to understand the nature of any runes, any ritualistic icons employed."

"But I can't remember all that," whined Bevin. "It was three-quarters of a century ago."

"Then we have a problem." Dru said the words quietly, but in the distance, thunder rolled in the cloudless sky.

His gaze darted to the window, then back to Dru's face. "I..."

"You cursed Richard Brook."

"Yes, but I didn't think it *meant* anything. I knew so little back then, and most of what we *thought* we knew was just hogwash. It wasn't until Aleister breached the barrier between this realm and Gehenna—"

"Yes, I'm aware of the breach," Dru said.

"Aleister! Aleister would know the details! His memories are intact, I hear, even after his death."

"That much is true," said Dru. "He's a judge, now. Did you know?"

"A judge?"

"Sure is, pal," said Leery. "And we've already talked to him, so you can abandon this farce to lead us down the proverbial path."

"But I'm not..." Gemble-Croix shook his head. "My mind is not what it once was. I'm old...and in ill health."

"Oh, I doubt that very much," said Dru. "Did you not know that I'm part succubus? Your illusions serve no purpose here, warlock."

Bevin coughed and looked at her wide-eyed. "But I'm a *Magnam Veneficus* of Mot! There are none more powerful."

"Keep on believing that, pal," said Leery with a harsh chuckle.

Dru sketched three silver runes, stitched them together with black lines, and tossed it casually toward the bed.

"Oh, how *dare* you!" screeched Gemble-Croix.

Dru yawned and looked at her nails as her rune set bit in and started chopping his illusion apart. Piece by piece the visage of the ancient creature fell away, revealing a man who looked to be middle-aged. His wispy silver hair turned black and thick, shrinking back into his head until it was nothing more than a black skullcap of tightly curled hair. His rheumy eyes changed next, become bright, focused, *alive*. Rather than the stained dressing gown, he wore black satin robes inscribed with silver runes.

"There, now," said Dru. "The real you."

Gemble-Croix shuffled to the side of the bed, a burning glare locked on Dru's face. "I will not be cast upon in my own home, young miss!"

Dru threw her head back and laughed.

"I'm getting the feeling that you've failed to grasp the situation, pal," said Leery. "But, please, keep right on doing what you're doing. I'm going to enjoying seeing Her Grace kick your ever-loving—"

"Ask your questions!" he snapped.

"Oh, boy," said Leery with a chuckle.

"I've already asked them," said Dru. "Answer them. Last chance."

"Frederick!"

"He's not coming."

"Fine! Yes, I cursed Brook, the bastard. Yes, I invoked a demon. Yes, I tasked it with—"

"Let's be clear," said Dru. "You *summoned* a Barghest from Gehenna?"

"Yes! Yes!"

"And then?"

"I tasked the Hell Hound—"

"*Barghest*!" snapped Dru.

"—with keeping a tally of Brook's evil-doings. I set a threshold and were Brook to surpass that upper limit of evil, I commanded the *Barghest* to punish him! I expected the curse to fire long ago! Long ago! Brook must have—"

"You summoned a creature you knew nothing about, gave it a vague set of commands, and—"

"I did *no such thing*! I explicitly commanded the demon—"

"Barghest," said Leery.

"—to keep track of—"

"*Evil-doings*? Don't make me laugh, fumbler," said Dru. "And *punish him*?"

"Yes! Yes!"

"Summon the Barghest."

"What? No! I do not—"

"Do it, Gemble-Croix, or you might find yourself explaining this to…someone else."

"You do know who her uncle is, don't you, pal?"

Bevin sneered, but his gaze did its darting dance between them. "I don't have the proper components. I don't have my apprentices. You can't expect me to perform such a complicated summoning—"

"Gregory," said Dru, and the floorboards creaked as the demon's weight settled on the floorboards.

"Your Grace?" Gregory's voice rumbled like an earthquake in process. "Does this fool threaten you?" He growled and took a single step toward the bed.

Gemble-Croix sat frozen, not even breathing, his gaze attached to Gregory as though the demon's fiery face held the secrets to life, the universe, and everything.

"No, Gregory. I was making a point. But stick around, I may have work for you."

Gregory straightened as much as he could in the room, though it did almost nothing to decrease the threat he seemed to generate. He glanced at Leery, nodded, and said, "Detective."

"Hiya, Gregory. How's things?"

"I'm well, thank you. Are you keeping to His Majesty's rules?" He arched a blackened eyebrow.

"With Her Grace as my minder? Of course, I am."

"Yes."

"You see, Gemble-Croix? Summoning from Gehenna is not such an ordeal."

He scoffed and narrowed his eyelids, but at Gregory's warning growl, his face went slack. "I... This kind of summoning is beyond me, Princess."

"Of course it is!" Dru snapped. "*Give me the name of the creature you summoned!*"

Gregory disappeared from where he stood next to Leery and reappeared crouching over the warlock not even a nanosecond later, his fire-tinged mouth open wide, his burning glare casting Gemble-Croix's face with an orange glow.

"Hey, call me a coffee bean if you want, but I'd start cooperating, Bevin."

The warlock tore his gaze away from the magma demon looming over him and sent a wide-eyed look of entreaty at Dru. "Nuh-name? I don't... That is, I..." He shook his head. "I don't know the beast's name." Gregory growled, and Gemble-Croix froze like a deer in headlights.

Dru leaned forward, cocking her head to the side. "You summoned a Barghest *unknown to you—*"

"If I'm honest, I didn't summon the creature. I only chanted the spell."

Dru rolled her eyes toward the ceiling. "It gets worse and worse. So, you *called* to a Barghest unknown to you and gave it an improperly defined task, then set it loose?"

The warlock dropped his gaze. "It was *seventy-eight* years ago. We didn't know much. We didn't even know of the Covenancy."

Gregory grunted and looked at Dru.

"How did you expect to recall this Barghest if you wanted to lift the curse?"

"I had no intention of lifting the curse. Ever. Brook was a fool and…and…and an asshole."

"I guess you'd know," said Leery.

Dru snapped her fingers and held out her hand. "The spell."

Gregory loomed closer and smiled, an expression more terrible than even his snarl.

Gemble-Croix froze once more, then dashed from the bed and crossed the room in a flash. He dug through the scrolls and books on the desk, flinging them to all sides, then raced to a bookcase next to the bed, then back across the room to another. He pulled books, glanced at them, then dropped them. He did this for a few moments, then he switched cases again and repeated the process. At last, he found an old leather-bound book. He turned and approached Dru with his head bowed, the book cradled before him like an offering. "Your Grace, the spell is inscribed in these pages. It was my personal spellbook at the time."

Dru snapped her fingers again. "Page."

Gemble-Croix nodded and spun the book around, flipping the cover open and pawing through the pages. When he found the page, he spun the book again, going down on one knee and holding the book out.

Dru glanced at it, her gaze flicking back and forth across the page, and while she did, her lips curled into a sneer. "Most of this is nonsense." She shook her head. "You're a fool, Gemble-Croix. Does the Temple of Mot know you're a fraud?"

He pulled his head back like an ancient turtle, the corners of his mouth drooping. "At the time, it was inspired. Spells like these were considered the height of supernatural manipulation."

Dru scoffed without looking up. "It's a wonder the Covenancy accepted you." She raised her eyes and narrowed her eyelids. "Then again, there was Aleister Crowley to consider."

Gemble-Croix sniffed. "Then surely I'm beneath your notice, *Your Grace.*" His lips twisted as the last two words flowed over them, and Gregory disappeared from the bed and reappeared looming over the kneeling warlock, his eyes and mouth glowing brighter with each hot breath, and Gemble-Croix growing paler and paler.

Dru reached out, cat-quick, and tore the page containing the spell from Gemble-Croix's grimoire. "I'm confiscating this," she said mildly, but then her eyes blazed crimson and her mouth curled into a snarl. "You are *forbidden* from contacting Gehenna, Bevin Gemble-Croix, by the power of my birthright. You shall despoil my subjects no longer!" A sound like that of a speeding freight train hammered at the windows, rattling the glass in their frames, and orange lightning blasted across the sky. Dru held up her hand, index finger extended toward the sky, head cocked, silken hair streaming down to her shoulder.

"I hear and witness, Your Grace," said Gregory in a reverent tone.

"Don't go anywhere, Bevin," said Leery. "When we find your Barghest, we'll have more questions, and if I have to chase you down, I'll be cross."

"Oh, there's no worry," said Dru. "He will never again walk any realm without the eyes of Gehenna on him."

"But-but-but—"

"I have spoken," said Dru. She rose to her feet, imposing and heroic, and stood over him. "Ignore my command at your peril."

"But I'm a *Magnam Veneficus* in the Temple of Mot! How am I to function?"

"Don't worry," Dru said in a sweet voice. "I'm sure that won't be a problem after Gregory reports to the *August Virtue*."

"What? I—"

"As you command," rumbled Gregory. He nodded to Leery and bowed to Dru. Then he was simply gone.

"Come on, Leery," said Dru.

Gemble-Croix paled and sank back on his butt. "This isn't fair..." he murmured.

"Hey, have you ever been to the fair? Everything there is rigged against you," said

SURE 'LOCK   87

Leery, rising slowly to his feet. "This seems a lot like the fair to me."

7

Leery sighed, leaned his head back against the headrest, and closed his eyes. Dru closed his door, then walked around to get in the driver's side. "Well, that was interesting," said Leery without opening his eyes.

"Those stairs were hard on you. I should have made him come down," said Dru. She turned the ignition, and the Crown Vic roared to life.

"Do we need surveillance on that joker?" asked Leery. "You know, to make sure he stays put?"

"No, I think I scared him so badly he won't leave the city. Besides, the Temple of Mot will be displeased with him for bringing their pathetic organization under Gehenna's scrutiny, so he probably won't step foot out of that room."

"Then that business about the 'eyes of Gehenna—'"

"Was completely true. Gregory will convey my orders back home. Unless that charlatan is a favorite of Mot's, no one will so much as bat an eye."

"But Luci had to enchant a silver cuff to make that stick with Dr. Agon." He stifled a cough and looked out the side window.

"Yes, but that was an enchantment. My command just means one of Gregory's brethren will track him from now on."

"Forever?"

Dru nodded once. "Forever." Her voice contained a note of finality as she slid the gear lever down into drive. "Now, I think, we should speak with Hinton, and if she hasn't found anything pointing at Brook's partners, we will return to Gehenna so I can show this nonsense to Uncle Luci and mother."

"Right."

"And you can take your nap."

Leery sighed, but this time, he didn't argue.

8

Dru and Leery rode the elevator up to the penthouse of the Sheffield and stepped into the palatial flat. Hinton, wearing her human disguise, lounged in one of the La-Z-Boy recliners, a stack of papers on her lap and a messy pile of discarded papers on the floor next to her.

"Oh, look, Dru. Such a delicate flower."

Hinton snorted. "I thought you died, wolfman."

"Yeah, well, Agon tried his best."

"He almost succeeded," said Dru.

A stricken expression flashed across Hinton's features, but it was gone in an instant. "I heard. Lucky for that scaled snake, Oriscoe has friends in the right places."

"And friends willing to risk everything," said Leery, his gaze locked on Dru.

"It was only a healing, Leery," she murmured.

"Yeah? Vinny told me what it did to you."

"You can't trust one of the Nephilim, Leery," said Jenn.

"Yeah, this one I can."

Silence fell among them for a minute, then Jenn flapped her hand at the papers scattered by her chair and said, "Mostly garbage. Silly little agreements between wanna-be mundanes and the great Richard Brook. Waivers of responsibility, nonsense like that. Nothing that rises to the level of a cantrip."

"Nothing about the partners?"

Jenn arched an eyebrow. "Nothing in the legal papers. Oh, his partnership agreement is here, but it's nothing exciting."

"But?" asked Leery.

Hinton smiled. "Can't get anything by your nose, can I, Comet?"

"I've missed you, too, Hinton. Spill it."

"Brook kept a journal of sorts. Mostly, he just complained about Myercough—"

"No, no," said Leery, "Myer—" and he coughed.

Hinton quirked an eyebrow at him. "Seriously?"

"Seriously," said Dru. "Goblin."

"Ah. That makes sense given some of the things in the journal."

"Like?"

"Come on, Hinton! Don't make us pull it out of you like some skell."

"Oh, please, Mr. Werewolf, don't hit me with a phone book."

"Then spill."

Jenn smirked at him. "Brook refers to 'that little rat-faced killer' on almost every page. He also talks about someone he calls 'sputum.' I'm guessing both of those are this Myer"—she coughed, sounding more like a shotgun going off than the cough of the delicate mundane she appeared to be—"for obvious reasons."

"They didn't get on?"

"It seems more like they hated one another. The goblin frequently stirred the shit pot about Brook's nighttime activities and habits. Brook called for numerous audits of the books, demanding to see everyone's billing sheets by way of revenge. I think he suspected Myer"—another booming cough—"was padding his hours."

"So, not as warm and fuzzy as they would have us believe," said Dru.

"And Brook made numerous references to 'the evidence' in the last three days. Unfortunately, he never said what it was."

"Why would anything be easy?" asked Leery with a sigh.

Hinton looked at him, her mouth open to zing some snark his way, but instead, she closed her mouth and looked at Dru, one eyebrow arched.

"We're getting through it," Dru mouthed. "Tired."

Hinton nodded. "I'll keep looking."

"Right," said Leery with a small, tired grin. "Don't let all that luxury get in your way."

"Too bad that dragon couldn't do something about your ability to speak," she said.

Leery grimaced at her, but he chuckled all the way back to the elevator.

9

Leery watched Dru circle around the front of the Crown Vic through slit eyelids. She stopped and got out her phone. She hit one of her contacts and glanced his way, but there was no way she could tell he was watching her—at least he didn't think there was.

"*Van Helsing,*" said Epatha over the phone.

"Hey, Lieu. It's Dru."

"*How's he doing?*"

Dru glanced his way again. "He's doing okay, but I think he's getting worn out. We've got something that needs checking on in Gehenna—"

"Ah. That's a good idea. Take him home and keep him there until tomorrow."

"That was my thinking. We need the information, anyway. Hinton found out that Brook and his partners weren't as lovey-dovey as they let on this morning."

"Mumbling cove magisters throwing the hatchet? That'll make a stuffed bird laugh if anything will. This information you need to check on in Gehenna…does it outweigh the partnership spat?"

"Outweigh? I don't know, but until we know more, it seems like it's on the same level."

"Hmm. No more sightings of the Barghest, by the by."

"That's good to know."

"Get him to Gehenna, Dru. Suggestionize he take easy the rest of the shift but don't let on. He's not up to dick, but he'd be poked up if he thought anyone knew. Tomorrow's time enough to confront the magisters."

"Thanks, Lieu."

"Not doing it for you, but you're welcome."

Dru nodded and disconnected, sliding her phone back into her bag. Then she threw another glance at Leery and continued around to get in.

"Eh?" he mumbled.

"Nothing, Leery. Nap if you can, we're off to Gehenna to check on this spell."

"Nah, I think we should go talk to the partners."

"I don't think—"

"I'm okay to sit in a magister's office and talk, Dru."

"Lieutenant Van Helsing wants us to find out about the summoning spell, first. She said tomorrow was time enough to confront the magisters."

"Yeah, I heard her," he said, opening his eyes.

Dru pursed her lips, and a little vertical line appeared between her brows. "Why don't I ever remember those ears of yours?"

He gave her a lopsided smile. "Oh, I think you do, Princess. When you really don't want me to hear, you go much farther away than the bumper of the car."

For the second time that day, her cheeks went pink. "Maybe."

SURE 'LOCK   95

"It's okay," he said and let his eyelids drift closed. "It gives me time to decide if I want to argue about it."

"And do you?"

"If I wasn't so tired, maybe."

Dru started the car. "Then we're going to Gehenna."

10

Dru stepped out of the fiery portal with Leery close behind. He had his tie loosened and his top button undone, but his gaze was bright. "Mother! Get some clothes on!" Dru called as she opened the ebony door and stepped out into the glistening obsidian hall.

"Okay, dear!"

Dru smiled at Leery. "That never gets old—having to tell her to get dressed when I bring someone by. She's in her throne room."

A look of wonderment washed over Leery's face. "I knew that. How did I know that, Dru?"

Dru smiled at him. "Welcome home, Leery."

"Uh, about the throne room…"

"Oh, right. No chairs," Dru muttered. "Can we meet you somewhere less formal, Mommy?" she cried, her voice rolling through the palace like thunder.

"Meet me in my dayroom, Dizzy!"

They strolled through the palace, keeping a slow pace, Leery loosing massive yawns every three or four minutes. But the air in the palace was cool and dry, and he enjoyed the peace and quiet.

When they reached the door to Agrat's dayroom, Dru knocked and said, "Dressed?"

"Of course, dear," said Agrat.

Dru opened the door and led Leery inside, taking him straight over to one of the plush chairs next to Agrat's worktable. Agrat's appearance matched her daughter's, which she acknowledged with a sly wink. When her gaze took in Leery's pallor, a vertical line appeared between her brows. "Drusilla! You've let him get over-tired! Luci will be distressed."

"Have you ever tried to train a kitten, Mommy?" Dru asked with a sigh.

"Hey, kittens are cute, right?" asked Leery.

"Yes, *kittens* are."

Agrat snapped her fingers, and a female demon of Gregory's race appeared bearing a

SURE 'LOCK 97

tray laden with raw meat and a bowl of steaming blood. "Transform, Leery. The fastest way to regain your strength is to feed your wolf."

"I..." He shook his head. "I'm not sure I can. I haven't since...since that night."

Agrat nodded. "You can. You are part of my family since your encounter with that snake, remember? The palace will lend you strength. Now, eat."

"Well..."

"Do what she says, Leery. Trust me, when she gets like this, it's go along or go deaf." Dru bent and started unbuttoning his shirt.

Agrat smirked. "Should I leave you two alone?"

"Very funny, Mommy," said Dru. She peeled his shirt and suit coat off as one flappy piece.

Leery shrugged and slipped out of his clothes, then began to transform. His wolf emerged as fast as winter molasses, but as the change progressed and the scent of the raw meat hit the olfactory centers in his brain, the sluggishness fell away. He fell on the tray of meat, a snarling mass of snapping teeth. Scar tissue tattooed his skin, and his once sleek fur had thinned to the point of balding in some places—especially around his head—and forming his *yarmulke* was a struggle. He looked much more the worse for wear than his human-half.

Dru reached for the bowl of hot blood, and he growled at her. She stepped back, a slight grin on her face.

Whoa! Settle down. She's our partner! Usually, the communication between them was rather one-sided, but this time, a thought intruded on Leery's human-half: *mate*.

"He's starving, the poor dear," said Agrat. "You can't hold it against him, Dizzy."

"I don't," she said. "I wasn't thinking."

He demolished the meat in a matter of minutes, then turned to the bowl of blood and nudged it toward Dru with his snout, ignoring his singed *payot* dragging through the gore left on the silver tray. He turned his chartreuse gaze on Agrat.

"More?" she asked.

Leery made a grunting bark.

Agrat snapped her fingers and another tray of meat arrived before the sound had faded. Dru sipped from her bowl of blood as though at a society tea party, and Leery bolted the meat down. When he finished the last scrap and had licked the tray noisily for at least a minute, he ducked his head at Agrat, then turned a sleepy gaze on Dru and yipped.

She smiled and nodded. "Curl up next to the fire," she said. "I'll ask Mommy about the spell."

With another tired yip, he walked stiffly to the fireplace rug, circled on it fifty or a hundred times, then lay down and curled up, his long tail wrapped around his legs. He let out a contented sigh and slept.

11

Leery woke at his leisure, luxuriating in the warmth, but stiff. He climbed to his four paws and set about stretching every muscle he had, moving with deliberation and care. With that accomplished, he shook himself and yawned. Already, his coat felt thicker than before his nap, and when he'd shaken his head, he'd glimpsed long, glossy *payot* instead of the charred nightmares he'd seen before.

He heard voices behind, rattling in that jarring tongue, the *Lingua Tenebris Lacuna*, the language of Dru's family. He turned and padded to the table, aware of Lucifer's assessing gaze and the warm look Agrat gave him. He stood next to his clothing and transformed—a much easier transformation than before. When it finished, he turned and found a chair next to Dru.

"You look better, Leery." Lucifer smiled at him across the table.

"Thanks, Luci. And thanks for the meal, Agrat."

A fleeting smile graced Agrat's lips, and her gaze bounced to Dru's for a moment. "Have I not said you are a son to me, Leery? Have I not promised to bring my legions, to *dance* for you myself, at your call? A plate or two of meat is nothing in comparison."

"Maybe so," Leery said with a shrug, "but it was the best meal I can remember. And, all of your promises aside, I'm still grateful."

She smiled at him sweetly.

"I don't know why I didn't think of it," said Lucifer. "From now on, you transform every night before bed and consume raw flesh."

"Uh...that wasn't..." Leery's gaze darted to Dru, and her bell-like laughter rang out.

"No, silly," she said. "That was kosher beef."

"Oh. Right," he said with red rising to his cheeks. "So, uh... What did we find out?"

"You mean this *spell* from Aleister's former companion?" asked Luci. "I'm not sure it worked."

"No?"

Agrat shook her head. "No. I gave your people magic. Formulas, methods. This follows none of them, and in their stead, it uses gibberish and symbols out of human imagination."

"But it could have worked?"

Luci shrugged his massive shoulders. "Perhaps. If the Barghest desired a summons to your realm, and if it *wanted* to stay there." He flicked the paper with a thick finger. "This isn't much of a contract. Very little to *compel* the Barghest's behavior, but it's possible one may have used the opportunity. Many of them are adventurous."

"Any way we can tell for sure?"

"I'll look into it," said the Lord of the Pit. "I have just the demon to set on the task."

Across the table, Agrat arched an eyebrow.

"Kasadya," said Lucifer.

Agrat smiled and nodded. "A good choice. Kokabiel would be another."

"Good. Kasadya will find this Barghest and report to you, Dru-baby." He cast a severe glance at Leery. "And you, my friend—"

"I feel much better," said Leery. "Ready to get back to it."

Agrat nodded. "That's the energy reserve from your wolf. Should you be required to transform and fight in that form, you will be weakened."

"Which is why you will transform and gorge every night," said Lucifer. "At least until your shifted-side is back to one hundred percent strength."

"Sounds like a prescription I can live with," said Leery.

"In the meantime, Dru-baby will continue her infusions, but"—Luci turned a stern gaze on his niece—"not to the point where *your* reserves grow shallow."

"What? Wait a minute..."

"Don't worry about it, Leery," said Dru, giving Lucifer the evil eye. "I have plenty of energy to spare and can refill my stores by drinking blood while you eat every night."

"Hey, I didn't sign up for energy infusions at your expense."

Dru shrugged and hit him with a one-sided smile. "Good thing I don't require your permission to make an essence gift."

"But—"

"Leery," said Agrat, "arguing with my daughter is senseless once she's made up her mind. Accept her gift gracefully."

"Well…" Leery sighed. "Thanks, Dru-baby." His grin stretched from ear to ear.

Lucifer lifted an eyebrow, but Agrat laughed.

"Uncle Luci, is it too soon to break both his legs?" asked Dru in a sugary-sweet tone.

12

The next morning at nine, Dru parked their cruiser in front of the triple bank of double doors that opened on the stern lobby of the Brook Tower on Wall Street. It was a severe heap of gray stone and darkened glass capped with a ziggurat of more gray stone. She and Leery got out and entered the lobby, the atmosphere of which gave every appearance of being either a library or a funeral home.

"Twenty-second floor," said Dru, glancing at the marquis. "I guess it would take the whole floor with one hundred seventy-nine magisters toiling away night and day."

"Right. It's a rough life. Say, how many corner offices do you think they have?" He held the elevator doors for her, then pressed the button for the twenty-second floor when she stepped in.

"Four?"

"Then why only three partners? Who gets the fourth corner?"

"That's a good question," said Dru in a musing tone. "But you know what?"

"What?"

"I think we're about to find out."

The elevator doors slid open on a staid space lined with marble and dark wood. The lobby was wide, with neat little groupings of leather couches and chairs. A tall counter stood opposite the elevator, and behind it, a waif-like fairy fluttered her wings and smiled.

"Welcome to Brook, Merris, and Myer"—she coughed into her fist—"a full-service firm. May I have the name of the magister you have an appointment with?"

"No appointment," said Leery. "We need to speak to Merris and Myer—" He coughed.

"Oh." The fairy's mouth made an O so perfect and her eyes grew so wide, the sight brought an amused grin to Leery's lips. "That is impossible."

"No, I think you'll find it's entirely possible," said Dru. "Tell them it's Detectives Nogan and Oriscoe."

"Oh!" The fairy went through her shocked-innocent routine again, then reached for the fairy-sized phone. "Are you sure? Mr. Myer"—she coughed—"gets very terse when I interrupt him."

"Call Merris, then," suggested Leery. "We could speak to him alone. At least, at first."

She cocked her head, smiled, and blinked about a million times in a single second. "Oh!" She dialed, then cupped a dainty hand over her mouth and murmured into the receiver. When she hung up the phone, she was all smiles. She beckoned, and they followed her around the wall separating the lobby from the rest of the firm.

The floor was set up in concentric rectangles, with single offices lining the outside walls, a ring of cubicles for associates, paralegals, and assistants to the magisters in the offices, and an inner rectangle that seemed dedicated to conference rooms, including an enormous square in the dead center of the floor. The receptionist led them to one of the smaller conference rooms.

"Can you help us with something?" asked Dru. "Three partners, and four corner offices. Who gets the fourth? An equity partner?"

"Oh, I'm not sure I know…"

"Come on, now," said Leery, hitting her with a brilliant smile. "You must know everything that goes on around here."

She blushed, and her wings fluttered. "Yes, well, I *do* see a lot." She leaned closer. "Mr. Myer"—she coughed into her dainty fist—"demanded two offices. One he uses for regular work, and the other…well, it's blocked off with tapestries and things. But my hearing is exceptional."

"I bet it is," crooned Leery.

"He chants spells in there," she said with a conspiratorial wink.

"Ah!" said Merris as he strode through the door. "Thank you, Glisandra. Could you arrange a coffee tray?"

"Of course, Mr. Merris." Glisandra nodded to Leery, then left, almost running, her dainty wings beating a mile a minute.

Merris smiled and waved them toward the comfortable looking chairs surrounding the table in the center of the room. "You have news already? That's impressive!"

"We haven't solved the case," said Dru. "But we have found out certain information…"

Leery leaned on the table, glanced both ways as though checking for eavesdroppers, then said, "Information from Richard Brook's private files at his residence—from a certain ledger…"

Merris shook his head and flopped his hands to show his palms. "I'm afraid I have no knowledge of what you're alluding to." He clasped his hands together in front of him.

"How did your other two partners get on? We got the impression that it was an amicable partnership," said Dru.

Merris smiled ruefully. "Well, all partnerships go through ups and downs. Brook, Merris, and Myercough is no exception."

"Hey! You didn't cough his name."

Merris hitched his shoulders. "When he's not around to complain, it's just easier."

"Good, that was getting silly. But what we're looking for goes a little beyond everyday disgruntlement," said Leery.

"Again," said Merris, "I have no idea what you are referring to."

"Did Brook ever mention a problem with your goblin partner's billing practices?" asked Dru.

"No."

"How about your own?" asked Leery. "Did he ever question your billable hours?"

Merris looked back and forth between them. "This is a chase of the proverbial goose, Detective. We're audited quarterly on our hours, and everything is triple-checked and confirmed."

"Then why would Brook think your little goblin friend was trying to cheat you? Why would he call for extra audits?"

Merris compressed his lips into a thin white line. "First of all, Detective Oriscoe, I find your comments distasteful. Vast is a goblin, that much is true, but not all goblins are cut from the same cloth. Is every cop the same as you? Is every werewolf?"

"Let's keep this focused on your partner," said Leery.

"Then quit disparaging him."

"Fine. I apologize if my comments were insensitive. Okay?"

Merris grunted, then turned to Dru. "I'd need to see this evidence to comment on it."

"That's fine," she said, "as we're only interested in whether your partner is cheating you as it relates to a motive for murder."

"For what?" demanded Merris. "*Murder*? Vast? Have you lost your minds?"

"He said it himself," said Leery.

"He said what himself?"

"At the precinct. He said if you two wanted to oust Brook, you could do it easily via the morality clause in your partnership agreement."

"I fail to see—"

"It's simple, Mr. Merris. If you could legally remove Richard Brook due to his proclivities and dining habits, then he could certainly remove either of you if you were cheating on your billing."

Merris stared at Leery in a cold fury, his hands clasped so tightly that his tendons bulged from his skin. Neither Leery nor Dru spoke, both watching him minutely. After a full two minutes, the magister began to relax, and the fury ebbed from his eyes. He gave them a single, slow nod, then said, "Point taken. But I think you are wrong to suspect Vast."

"Is it true he keeps a ritual room in one of the corner offices?"

Merris blinked, then glanced over his shoulder at the far corner office. "Well, yes, but our practice is a busy one, and none of us have time to—"

"Meeting with clients? Lunching with them? Those activities keep you too busy to cast spells from home?"

The magister swallowed. "Me? No. Vast spends much of his time here, though. He's almost always in the office."

"No life, huh?" asked Leery.

"Quite the opposite, but his life is this firm."

"Then it's likely he would respond poorly to a threat to the firm," said Dru. "Or his place in it."

"Well..."

"You know, if someone had the goods on him and wanted to use them to oust him from his two corner offices."

Merris cocked his head and frowned. "So would I. So would Richard."

"I see," said Dru. "Would Richard go so far as to *fabricate* evidence of misconduct against Myercough?"

"Richard could be vindictive and petty, but something like what you mention seems out of character."

"Maybe for his modern persona," said Dru. "We've heard differently about his younger self."

Merris shrugged.

"Let's turn to another matter," said Leery.

"It's your meeting."

"Do you think Myercough has the magical chops to summon a Barghest?"

"Vast commands powerful magic, but summoning is not one of his talents."

"No?" asked Dru.

With a shake of his head, Merris said, "He's a sorcerer."

"Ah," she said. "He forecasts the market?" She quirked her eyebrow.

Merris blushed and looked down at the table. "Vast does lead the team that attempts to gauge market forces and—"

"Via divination," said Dru.

"I don't know as I'd call it—"

"Come, Mr. Merris. Let's stop playing games."

"I'm not comfortable speaking for Vast in this matter. I'll call him to join us." Merris glanced through the glass walls at a young vampire sitting nearby and jerked his chin toward the southeast corner office. The woman nodded and scurried toward it.

"Fine," said Leery. "In the meantime, how's that client list coming?"

"What? You still need it? I assumed—"

"Every stone, Mr. Merris."

"Uh, right. I'll have to check."

"And the executor of Brook's will?" asked Dru.

"Yes. Vast did find that out. It's a small family firm in Brooklyn. I believe the executor is a woman named Lena Cassidy."

"Small world," said Leery, darting his gaze to meet Dru's.

Myercough came stomping from his office, his brows drawn together in a stormy expression, and his fists clenched by his sides. He flung the glass door open. "What's this, Merris?" he demanded. "I'm *busy*! You *do* remember the Sawgrass merger?"

"Vast, the police have questions."

The goblin arched a craggy eyebrow. "So? Answer them, Merris! What good are you if I have to do *everything* around here?"

"It will only take a few minutes," said Leery. "Your partner is squeamish when it comes to admitting you are divining the future of the stock market."

Vastalan turned his head slowly, pulling his angry stare from Merris's face and transferring it to Leery's. "Be careful, Detective," he hissed coldly. "Defamation suits can be financially devastating, even when defended successfully."

"Oh, look, Dru. Threats," Leery said in a bored tone.

"I agree. I wonder if one of these fine magisters knows the sentence associated with intimidating a law enforcement official."

"I bet they do, Dru. If they don't, they could always Gurgle it."

"Google, you fool!" snapped Vast. "And as entertaining as your bit of theater is, I made no threats. I merely explained how defamation suits can ruin a fellow."

"Sit down, Myer—" Leery coughed and pointed at an empty chair.

Myercough turned halfway back toward the outer office, then pivoted on his heel and took a seat. "Make it quick!" he snapped. "I'm only doing this to curtail further interruptions, but I warn you: my patience has limits!"

"Understood," said Dru. "Merris says you lack the power for summoning entities from other realms."

"It isn't beyond my *power*, dear girl. It's beyond my *interest*. I am a sorcerer. I commune with entities in other realms hourly and command them to speak. It's how I collect business intelligence."

Dru nodded. "And I imagine you pay particular attention to transdimensionals?"

Vast lifted a shoulder and flopped his hand. "And why not?"

"Nothing illegal about that," said Merris.

"Like we said, we don't care," said Leery. "We're only trying to solve Richard Brook's murder. Speaking of that, is it true he was trying to remove you from the firm?"

Myercough's entire visage contorted with fury. "Lies! Manufactured garbage!"

"Can you prove that?" asked Merris in a quiet voice, and Myercough shifted his glare to him.

"Do I need to?"

Merris grunted.

SURE 'LOCK

"Even if it's all lies," said Leery, "we understood you would react badly to the threat."

"Well, why not? Wouldn't you?" His gaze danced back and forth between Leery and Dru. "If someone created a bunch of lies about you and tried to use them to ruin you, to ruin your life?"

"Sure," said Leery. "I might even be tempted to kill the guy."

Myercough scoffed. "I can believe that of you, but few could believe it of *me*. It's true Brook was trying to run me off in a half-hearted manner, but he would have failed. I have more evidence against him, and the arbitration would have gone my way if he chose to pursue it. I didn't need him dead."

"So you say," murmured Merris, his gaze resting on the table in front of him.

"Yes, Merris," said Vast wearily. "So I say."

"And this evidence you have against him?" asked Dru. "What is its nature?"

"I've told you already," said Myercough with a sigh. "The women. The essence stealing."

"Turns out all that was legal," said Leery. "But I bet you already knew that."

The goblin pressed his lips together and glared across the table.

"Right. So, here's what we're going to do," said Leery in an authoritative voice. "You are going to get *all* the evidence you've accumulated, and we're going to see how it matches up with what we've found. *And*"—he switched his gaze to Merris—"your partner here is going to leave us right now and go fetch it. He's also going to get us copies of all the billing sheets for your firm. We're taking them with us and giving them to a team of forensic accountants." He pinned Myercough to his seat with a fierce glare. "You're going to stay with us while he does that. Sound good?"

Myercough sneered but shrugged. "In my upper drawer on the left, Merris. It's marked with Richard's name." Merris left the room, almost at a jog. "I wouldn't kill Richard. *Couldn't* have killed him. Not with a Barghest, at any rate. I'm a sorcerer, not a warlock."

Leery nodded. "Sure, we get that. But I bet you know at least one of those fixers we talked about yesterday. Or maybe you have friends in the Redcaps."

"Again, with the Redcaps! I am *not* affiliated with the Redcaps!"

"Sure, sure," said Leery. "Hey, *we* believe you, but our lieutenant is a real stickler. She insists we verify *everything*."

"And how can you verify a negative, Detective?"

Leery pursed his lips. "Hey, that's a good point. You must be a magister or something."

Myercough slumped against the back of his chair. "I had nothing to do with Richard's demise."

"See, that's something our lieutenant will want us to verify."

Myercough scoffed and turned his head away. "If you have nothing else?"

"No, I think you should stay here with us until Mr. Merris comes back."

"Fine," said Myercough with a sigh. "Fine."

13

Leery got up and wandered toward the squad's coffee machine. If there was one thing he hated, it was poring through financial paperwork. If there was one thing he hated even more than that, it was watching a bunch of forensic accountants on loan from 1PP stare at the same paperwork. He got a mug of coffee and strolled back, glancing at the vending machine in the hall.

"No," said Dru without looking up.

"I was just looking."

"You're not going to fill up on that junk. You have a real lunch coming."

"I do?"

"Yes," she said. "Gregory is bringing it."

Leery opened his eyes wide, then took a furtive look around. "It's not dinner time."

"No, and don't worry. It's not *that* meal. My father decided to cook you lunch."

"Hercule?"

"He's a phenomenal chef by all accounts. He *is* French."

"Right." He strolled around the squad room, making a full circuit before coming back to his desk. "You know, I could—"

"Why don't you call Jathy?"

"Yeah, she didn't seem all that happy to hear from me yesterday." He sank into his desk chair and reached for the phone. "Hey, have you heard anything from—"

"Invite her to lunch. Here." Dru looked up from the stack of papers in front of her. "And, yes, Kasadya found several Barghest missing. He's working on narrowing it down to unlicensed summonings." She flicked her fingers at his phone. "Tell Jathy my father will be here. That should motivate her."

"Uh...yeah." Dru stared at him until he reached for the phone and dialed Jathy's number. His daughter picked up on the second ring. "Hey, Jathy. It's Dad."

"I was sleeping," she groused.

"Yeah, sorry. How are you feeling? I bet 'drained' is a good word."

"Ha-ha."

"Hey, if a dad can't use dad-jokes, who can?"

"I'm okay, Dad. Really. You don't have to worry."

"But you can see why I do, right?"

She sighed, a string of explosions over the phone line. "Dad..."

"Hey, no judgment involved, kiddo. It's a serious question—you get why your mother and I feel a little..."

"Yes, Daddy," she said and yawned. "But is the reverse true? You're a... You are what you are. You live in the otherworld every day. You see things I can only imagine. Magic. Angels. Dragons."

"Yeah, let's leave that last one off the list of things to do on bring-your-daughter-to-work day."

"Yeah... Uh, I didn't know about all that until I talked to Mom last night. I wouldn't have... It's just—"

"It's okay, Jathy. We both have let things slide too far."

"Um, yeah."

"And listen, how about coming down here for lunch? I've got a great lunch lined up. French food by a terrific chef you might have heard of—"

"I don't know, Dad."

"His name is Hercule DuSang."

The line rang with silence for half a minute or so.

"Are you kidding?"

"Would I kid you, kid?"

"In the dictionary, under the term 'hell yes' is your picture."

"Well, that's probably true, but what I meant was would I kid you about *this*?"

"Mom said your new partner is...*special*?"

He looked at Dru and grinned. "You could say that."

"Dad...you sound...*happy*."

SURE 'LOCK 121

"Yeah, Jathy, I suppose I am."

Dru arched an eyebrow at his stare, his sappy grin. He shook his head and waved her back to her paperwork.

"That's… Dad, that's good. You deserve to be happy."

"So do you, Jath. You and your sister."

"I'm not up yet, Daddy. I hope your lunch isn't anytime soon. If I'm going to meet Hercule DuSang and Drusilla DuSang—"

"Uh, that's Drusilla bat Agrat."

"Oh, right. I forgot Gehenna is a civilized matriarchal society."

"Maybe don't bring that up with Hercule."

She chuckled. "I'm sure he knows, Daddy."

"Yeah, I am too, but every man has pride."

"Can I talk to him? About what I want, I mean."

An icy clump dropped into Leery's guts. "Kid, you can talk to anyone you like. Even if I call you a kid, and maybe treat you like one, you're a grown woman. But don't be surprised if he doesn't react as you might expect. He, too, has a daughter."

"Oh."

"But talk to him all you want, Jathy. Ask him about what it means to be undead. Ask him if he would recommend it."

"I will. What time?"

"Oh...right." He cupped the phone's microphone with his hand. "When will Hercule be here?"

Dru glanced at her watch. "Whenever we want. Gregory will bring him. Should we send Gregory for her first?"

He took his hand away from the phone. "How long do you need to get ready?"

"An hour," she said.

"Okay. Be downstairs and look for the big black SUV that looks like a tank from some sci-fi movie."

"What?"

"You'll understand when you see it." He said goodbye and hung up, grinning all the while.

14

Jathy shared a brownstone off West 112th Street with a couple of high school girlfriends. None of them had gone to City College and then on to Columbia, like they'd yammered on about while convincing their parents to foot the bill for a Morningside Heights address.

Gregory drove like a man possessed by demons, the SUV's engine shrieking and wailing as he hammered the accelerator through the turn onto 112th Street from Frederick Douglass Boulevard, scattering pedestrians left and right. The vehicle's big tires added to the cacophony while at the same time adding smoke to the City's natural bouquet.

Jathy stood on the sidewalk, gawping at the monstrous vehicle as it slewed back and forth across the entire width of the street. She stood frozen as the SUV skidded to a halt in front of her, eyes wide, mouth agape.

Leery opened the rear door and hopped out, with Dru sliding out behind him. "Jathy!" he said, throwing his arms wide for a hug.

"What… How did… Daddy!" she stammered. "That thing is…"

"Cars are different in Gehenna," said Dru, stepping around Leery. "I'm Dru."

Jathy tried to bow and curtsey at the same time, then gave up both and ducked her head to hide her blazing cheeks. "Princess! I mean, Your Majesty, I'm—"

"The correct form of address in a formal setting would be 'Your Grace,' but we are not in a formal setting. Call me Dru." She smiled warmly at her and stepped in close to give her a hug.

"I..."

"Relax, Jathy," said Leery. "It takes a minute to realize she's just a woman, same as you."

Jathy's gaze zipped up to the curved horns sprouting from Dru's head, then she shook her head.

Dru chuckled. "You'll get used to them." She linked her arm through Jathy's. "Now, let's get going. I'm starving!"

"Oh, sorry, I—"

"You're going to have to stop that," said Dru with a smile. "If we're to be friends."

"Friends?"

"Of course."

"But I'm a nobody... A wanna-be..."

"Nonsense. You're Leery's daughter, and that makes you *somebody* in my world. Someone *special*. And even if you weren't Leery's kin, you're not a nobody, you're only young." She drew her closer to the SUV and opened the front passenger side door. "Come,

SURE 'LOCK

meet Gregory. He's served my family for…well, forever. Gregory, this is Jathy Oriscoe, Leery's daughter."

He turned his face toward her and nodded. "Mistress," he said in formal tones. He was in his humanoid form, dressed in black with his chauffeur's cap tilted back on his head and slightly askew.

Jathy's eyes grew very wide when she saw the orange glow from deep in his throat. "Oh! I mean, hello!" She held out her hand.

"Hello," said Gregory with a formal bow of his head. "Your mother must be beautiful."

Jathy blushed.

"Because you certainly didn't get your looks from your father."

"Hey!" said Leery and then grinned.

"But," Gregory went on, "if you got his courage and sense of duty, you must be quite a woman."

Jathy glanced at Leery and raised an eyebrow. "I definitely got his stubborn streak."

Gregory laughed, a deep booming sound that rattled windows and set off car alarms all around. "I will remember that."

Dru ushered Jathy into the back of the SUV, then got in beside her. Leery took the front seat and grinned at Gregory like a kid with a new bike.

"Daughters are wonderful creatures," the magma demon said in a low tone.

"You've got that right," said Leery.

"Ready, Your Grace?" asked Gregory. Dru pointed to Jathy's seat belt, and after she clipped it on, she nodded. Gregory hammered the accelerator, and the big black SUV took off as though pursued by a legion of zombies—and not the slow, lumbering kind, either. Jathy latched onto the grab handle with one hand and Dru's forearm with the other, her face pallid, her eyes wide.

Dru laughed. "It's okay. Gregory is a transdimensional."

"Um... What does that mean, exactly?"

"He can be in many different places or times at once," said Leery from the front seat. "He's a good driver. You can relax." Only his death grip on the grab handle above his door belied the conviction of his tone.

Gregory glanced at him and chuckled.

15

A moment after Gregory dropped Jathy, Dru, and Leery on the sidewalk outside the Twenty-seventh Precinct, Gregory once again screeched up to the curb, this time depositing Hercule and a few insulated boxes on the sidewalk. He disappeared with the SUV, then reappeared and picked up the boxes.

Jathy stared at him, and he smiled at her.

"Transdimensional," he said. "Remember?"

"Now I get it."

"Leery, *mon ami*, who is this lovely young woman?"

"Hercule, meet my daughter, Jathy Oriscoe. Jath, meet Hercule DuSang, Dru's father and all-around good guy."

Hercule nodded at Leery, then bowed over Jathy's proffered hand. "It is a pleasure to make your acquaintance, *ma beauté*."

Jathy blushed with pleasure but then paled, and her gaze darted to the noontime sun shining above their heads. "The sun! Aren't you…"

Hercule chuckled. *"Non, non, chère fille.* Nothing to worry about. Not everything in the stories is true."

"Then the sun doesn't..."

"Turn me to ash?" He showed her a kind smile. "Maybe once... But these days, we have sunscreens, melanin treatments, things of this nature. Plus, my power has grown over the years."

"Oh," she said. "You can do magic, too?"

Once again, he showed her a kind smile. "It is said *ma meilleure magie*—my best magic—occurs in the kitchen."

"Come on, folks," said Leery, jogging to the door and holding it open. "We don't want Hercule's efforts to go to waste, do we?"

They trooped to the elevator and rode it to the second floor. Leery led them to a small break room shared by the Supernatural Inquisitors Squad. He took one of the boxes from Gregory and set it on a table that ran along one wall, then motioned for Gregory to do the same.

"Coffee, anyone?" he asked.

"I have taken it on myself to brew you a wonderful *rôti français, mon ami.* But be aware this is no *café américain.* I have prepared the

SURE 'LOCK 129

café in the proper way." He turned and waved a hand at Gregory. "Unpack." He returned his gaze to Leery. "*Mais où est ton charmant lieutenant?*"

"I'll go get her, Daddy," said Dru. "Leery is to sit and rest." She gave him a stern look. "Is that understood?"

Leery flashed a sardonic grin and moved to the table in the center of the room.

"I said, *sit and rest.*"

Hercule chuckled. "*Croyez-moi, mon bon ami,* it would be best to do as my daughter says."

"Yeah, yeah," said Leery, sinking into one of the chairs, and with a final stern glance, Dru turned and left.

"Wow," said Jathy with a smile. "I've never seen you so docile, Daddy."

"And you, Jathy Oriscoe. Sit with your father while Gregory and I prepare *le repas.*"

She glanced at Leery and twisted her fingers. "Actually, Mr. DuSang—"

"*Mais non!* I must be Hercule to the daughter of my great friend."

Jathy dimpled. "Hercule, I'm very interested in—"

"After the food, *mon chère. Ma fille,* Drusilla, has told me of your interests in my kind. There will be plenty of time for questions, *ça je te le promets.*" He waved his hand toward the table. "Sit. Speak with your father who loves you."

She smiled and ducked her head, moving to the table and sitting next to Leery. "Did you arrange this?" she murmured.

Leery cocked his head to the side. "I'd choose differently for you, Jath, but I'd rather you learn the facts from a trustworthy source than go on as you have been."

"But I thought werewolves and vampires didn't get along."

"It's true that some on both sides harbor resentments and prejudice from the War of Fangs. Hercule is a bigger man."

"Your father has taught me to be," called Hercule from the table where he and Gregory were busy unloading the boxes.

Jathy turned her probing gaze on her father. "You...seem different, Daddy."

He shrugged. "I suppose I am different, Jathy. When I was... When I became as I am, I didn't understand a lot of things about living as a werewolf. It's a balance. Wolves are hierarchical creatures, and if there's room at the top, they try to dominate. It took a while for me to realize that and achieve a balance with my other side."

Dru came in, and Epatha Van Helsing floated in behind her. She nodded to Leery, and when she saw Jathy, she came straight over. "Hello," she said. "I'm Epatha Van Helsing. I'd offer to shake, but, well, I'm a creature of the spirit realm."

"Pleased to meet you," said Jathy.

Epatha turned and bowed. "Monsieur DuSang, Gregory, it's a pleasure to see you both. Welcome to the Two-Seven."

Hercule strode over, wiping his hands on a small towel. "My dear Lieutenant Van Helsing," he said, smiling. "It is *our* pleasure."

"Aren't they..." began Jathy. Then she blushed a bright crimson.

Epatha turned to her and smiled. "Names aren't everything." She nodded at Dru. "Besides, working alongside Dru has taught me a thing or two about vampires that my family didn't know."

"You must join us!" said Hercule.

Van Helsing smiled. "I will sit with you, but I can't partake."

Hercule smiled. "I had hoped you would be here. I brought something for you, specially prepared by His Majesty, *mon beau-frère*. He sends greetings, best-wishes, and inquires when you might visit him again."

Gregory stepped up and lifted a sterling silver cover off a matching tray. "Undifferentiated ectoplasm," he rumbled.

Epatha arched an eyebrow at Dru. "My, my," she said. "A simple Victorian girl could get to like this butter upon bacon. If I hadn't met your lovely wife, I might think you a gal-sneaker. Please say hello to Her Majesty for me and convey my best wishes. As for your brother-in-law, you must thank him for me. Please convey my regrets—I don't think I'm up to another portal crossing so soon after the last."

Hercule snapped his heels together and gave her a half-bow. "I will convey your sentiments. Now"—he swept his hand toward the table—"please grace us with your presence. All is in readiness."

Van Helsing glided toward Leery and rested her insubstantial hand on his shoulder for a moment, then floated through the table and took a seat across from him. Gregory moved around the table and set the bowl of undifferentiated ectoplasm in front of her with a bow.

"Would you care for a glass, as well?"

"No need," said Epatha, dipping her forefinger into the bowl. "I couldn't lift it anyway."

"And now," said Hercule as he came toward the table with a covered silver tray, "your lunches are served." He lay the tray on the table and swept away the lid. Inside lay a pile of Croque-Monsieur, gleaming yellow with buttery goodness and dripping gruyere cheese and caramelized French ham.

"Oh, boy," said Leery. "I'm suddenly salivating, Hercule."

The elder vampire smiled. "And don't forget the *café*," he said as Gregory brought the insulated carafe to the table and poured three small cups and two giant mugs full of the ebony goodness. Hercule sat and took one of the mugs. He glanced at Jathy over the rim. "Another fine thing your father has taught me."

Grinning, Leery took the other mug and drank a long draught. He set the mug down and smacked his lips. "Now, *that's* what I call coffee. It's even better than the stuff Puriel gave me."

Hercule flashed a thin smile at him. "*Mais bien sûr!*"

16

After they ate, Epatha begged off and disappeared into the hall. Leery stood and stretched, then bent and kissed Jathy on the cheek. He nodded to Dru and said, "We've got to get back to it, Jath. Thank you for coming down. Gregory and Hercule will see you home."

Hercule bowed his head. "*Ce serait mon honneur,* Leery. I will ensure her safety to the same extent that you have risked ensuring the safety of mine."

"Thanks, but let's hope you don't run into any dragons on the way to Morningside Heights."

"We will not," said Gregory. "This I swear."

Leery grinned and slapped him on the shoulder. "I'd expect no less."

Jathy stood and wrapped her arms around Leery. "Thank you," she whispered.

Smiling, Dru led Leery into the hall. As they walked out, Jathy turned to Hercule. "Did Dru tell you I was interested in the Dead Set?"

"*Mais non!* That will not do, Jathy. They are a dishonorable bunch. Permit me to tell you of my race…"

Dru and Leery walked into the squad room, and she bumped him with her shoulder. "It's a good thing, Leery," she said. "You're a fine father."

"You're right on the first part, at least." He glanced at the paperwork on his desk, then shuffled all the reports and papers into a messy stack. He grabbed Dru's bunch as well, then walked across the squad room and dropped them on the desk of one of the forensic accountants who'd chosen the wrong moment to take a break. "Come on, Dru. Let the experts wade through this crap. I want to head out to Brooklyn. I've got a question or two for Lena Cassidy."

Dru shrugged and grabbed her things. "You can nap on the way over."

"Nah. I'm a little sleepy from all that expresso your dad calls *café*, but I'm fine."

"Sleepy from expresso?" Dru shook her head. "Then I'll give you another boost in the car."

"In broad daylight?"

She grinned at him and tossed a wink over her shoulder. "If you're good."

They stepped into the elevator, and Leery said, "Listen, I appreciate the essence transfer and everything, Dru, but I don't want to—"

"Leery?"

"Yes?"

"Dear one?"

"Uh-huh?"

"Shut it."

"Yes, Dru."

"That's better." The elevator doors opened, and they crossed the lobby and headed out into the street.

A parking enforcement officer was staring at Hercule's SUV, thick ticket book out. Shaking his head, Leery walked over to him and said, "Nah."

The officer looked at him and quirked an eyebrow. "Nah, what?"

"You don't want to end your career, right? You don't want to have to go back to bussing tables or whatever it was you did before someone made the mistake of giving you that pad, right?"

"Uh..."

"Right." He lay his arm across the officer's shoulders. "Listen, kid. This SUV belongs to a high-muckity-muck."

SURE 'LOCK 137

"Who?"

"Royalty, pal. Her father"—he hooked his thumb at Dru—"and a *personal* friend of mine."

The parking enforcement officer sniffed and flipped his pad closed. "He *is* double-parked in front of a police station."

"That's where you've got it wrong. *He's* not double-parked, this guy at the curb is just in his spot."

"Uh…"

"No, trust me on this. If you see this badass SUV parked upside down on top of an ambulance in the emergency department's unloading zone, you give the ticket to the ambulance. If you see this SUV, I don't know, parked on the steps of the federal courthouse with bodies scattered all around, you write him a thank you card. Capisce?" Leery flapped his coat open and let the afternoon sun wink on his golden detective sergeant shield.

The officer glanced at it and put his ticket book away. "Whatever you say, Detective."

"There's a good lad," said Leery with a smile. He fished out a business card. "I like you, kid. You run into any problems on the job, you give me a call."

"So, what? You're offering to be my rabbi?"

Leery shrugged. "We'll see how it goes." He turned and walked with Dru to their cruiser.

"You're in a good mood this afternoon."

"She *hugged* me, Dru. Plus, your father makes the best Croque-Monsieur I've ever had. And his coffee's to die for."

"Just think, not a single drop of holy water went into the pot," Dru said with a wry lilt in her voice.

17

Leery almost bounced up the steps to Lena Cassidy's front door. He thumped the door with the side of his hand, then grinned at Dru as she stepped up beside him. She bumped him with her shoulder and grinned back.

"I told you that you'd feel better," she said.

"Yeah. I... Anyway, thanks for the invigoration spell. Just don't be so worried about my energy that you drain yourself, okay?"

"It's okay, Leery. If I get a little low, I'll just do this"—she turned and cast a bawdy gaze on him and ran her tongue across her lips—"and take some of it back."

Leery's knees felt weak, and his pulse slammed into high gear. "Yeah. Um…" He lost his train of thought. "I…" His throat dried like a splash of water in the Sahara. "That's just…"

She wrinkled her nose at him and grinned. "Nice to know you're still interested."

"I…" He shook his head and looked around as though he had no idea where they were. "That is…" The door opened, and Samuel gazed out at them. Leery glanced at him and said, "Uh… Hi. I'm Detective Nogan and this is Detective Or—"

Dru put a hand on his arm. "Don't mind Detective Oriscoe, here"—she patted his arm—"he was injured recently and is a little confused, but it will pass. We need to speak with Ms. Cassidy, again."

"I shall inquire," said Samuel with a snooty sniff as he looked down his long nose at Leery.

"Oh! I remember you!" said Leery.

"And there's no need to inquire," said Dru. "We'll save time by coming with you. It's important, and it's about Richard Brook."

The butler sniffed again but opened the door wider. "You know where the sitting room is. Go there, and Ms. Cassidy will join you at her leisure." He glanced at Leery. "Perhaps that will provide the required time for the senility to improve." He turned his back and walked to the staircase and began to ascend, moving so smoothly that it appeared his legs didn't connect to the rest of him.

Leery and Dru walked into the formal parlor with the pink grand piano. "That was mean," said Leery.

"Yes, it was," said Dru, "but it was a lot of fun, too. And I've had to be so good since your injury."

Leery grinned and walked to the wall containing a bunch of paintings. "I'm going to be over here, pretending I know anything about these cartoons."

"Cartoons? I think that one in the middle is Renoir. *Sleeping Woman*, if I'm not mistaken."

"Should've called it *Peeping Tom and the Bare-Chested Lady*."

"And that one," said Dru, pointing at a canvas hung near the ceiling, "that's Titian's *Venus, Mars, and Eros*."

SURE 'LOCK 141

"Or, as it's better known, *Man Kissing Naked Lady While A Random Cherub Takes Snapshots*."

Dru laughed. "I don't think Eros would like you calling him a random cherub."

"Or a cherub, for that matter," said Lena Cassidy from the doorway.

"Nice, uh, art," said Leery, turning to face her.

"Thanks," said Lena with a mocking smile. "My collection is worth more than you will make in your lifetime."

"Hey, don't bet on it. I'm going to take up clogging one of these days and get famous."

"Clogging?" asked Lena, lifting one eyebrow.

"Sure. It's going to take off one of these days, you watch and see. When it does, look me up, and maybe I'll come dance at one of your froufrou parties. You'll be the envy of everyone in town."

Lena smiled and shook her head. "Maybe you should put your energy into writing. You've got quite an imagination."

"You think so?" asked Leery. "Sometimes I wonder. For instance, I can't imagine why you neglected to tell us you were Brook's executor yesterday."

Cassidy lost her smile and glanced at Dru. "Maybe you should remain a cop instead of taking up any of the arts."

Leery shrugged. "It's a gift. But that doesn't answer my question, does it?"

"Did you ask a question?"

"Why didn't you share that bit of—"

"Magister-client privilege!" snapped Lena.

"—information?" finished Dru.

"And don't start with that magister-client crap," said Leery with a scoff. "We all know your position as executor is not subject to privilege."

Cassidy shrugged. "You didn't ask."

"We didn't *ask*? Hear that, Dru? We were supposed to ask."

Dru fixed Cassidy with a hard stare. "Okay, allow me to run through all the obvious things you should share with us—"

"Make sure to phrase them as questions," said Leery. "Evidently we've drifted into an episode of Jeopardy."

Lena snickered and moved across the room to the bar behind the pink piano. "Drink?"

"No, thanks," said Leery. "We just ate lunch."

She set about mixing an elaborate cocktail that included seven liquors, three kinds of juice, a splash of hot sauce, a cube of sugar, and an umbrella stabbed through an olive—all in a sixteen-ounce glass. "Yes, I'm Richard's executor. My family has handled the Brook family's estate matters since Augustus was a pup."

"Yeah, but let me ask you an important question," said Leery.

"That's what you're here for."

"What in the Nine Realms *is* that?"

Lena swirled the concoction in her tall glass and smiled at him. The smile didn't reach her eyes, however, which looked as though they'd better serve a crocodile. "I call it 'a bunch of shit in a glass that will get me drunk fast.'"

"Oh. I've heard of that," said Leery. "It was the sugar cube that threw me."

"Laced with LSD," she said after taking a gulp.

"In for a penny," said Leery. "But I guess we'd better ask our questions in a hurry."

Lena shrugged and took another gulp.

"I assume you are familiar with the will? Who are Brook's beneficiaries?"

"Do you want the whole list?"

"In for a penny," repeated Leery.

"And the awards, if you know them," said Dru.

"Fine. The beneficiaries are Megan Moorehouse, who gets a one-dollar lease of the Brooklyn house for the balance of her natural life, Maribel Ibzia, who gets a one-dollar lease of the Sheffield flat for thirty years—"

"Huh. The little vamp was telling us the truth, Dru."

"Will wonders never cease?" asked Dru in a droll voice.

"—Richard's cousin, Marcus Brook, gets the two properties at the end of the lease terms. I get most of Richard's liquid holdings, and one of his partners gets his stock portfolio, including his shares of the firm."

"So, the little goblin has another motive."

Lena shook her head. "The other one."

"The other motive? I think what he had on Brook is a wash against what Brook had on him."

"What? No. The other *partner*."

"Merris?" asked Dru, and Lena nodded.

"Wait a minute. Did you say *you* get all his liquid assets?"

Lena lifted her chin and shook her hair out of her face. "And why not? Richard and I—"

SURE 'LOCK   145

"You broke up over two months ago, and he didn't take you out of the will?"

She lifted her shoulders, then looked down at her drink and swirled it before taking another huge gulp. "We are—*were* talking. We broke up for silly reasons. He wanted to get back together, to marry me."

"Do you have proof of those conversations?"

She flapped her hand. "You can pull my phone records to confirm the calls. As for their content, it was only Richard and me on the line."

"That's pretty convenient, isn't it?" asked Dru.

"Well, since you asked me that question, in that tone, and I can't refute your implication, no. As a matter of fact, I find it *highly inconvenient*. This conversation will repeat itself—at least with Marcus, Megan, and Maribel, but I'm willing to bet that greedy wizard will want to grill me, too."

"Merris?" asked Leery.

"Who else?"

"Greedy?"

"Yes, and before you ask: yes, he's a wizard."

"Cute," said Leery with a frown.

"No, not really. He's too plain. And rank greed is hardly attractive. Plus, he's a real asshole. So demanding, so cranky."

"Are you sure you're not confusing him with Myercough? The goblin?"

"And Merris gets his stocks *and* shares in Brook, Merris, and Myercough?" asked Dru.

"Bingo," said Lena.

"Hey, there's no need to start name-calling," grumbled Leery.

"What?"

"Don't mind him," said Dru. "How much?"

"She means how much do you stand to get if we convict Merris?" Leery said after a moment.

"What? I don't—"

"Save it," said Leery. "Answer our questions."

Lena shrugged, her gaze creeping up to the paintings lining the wall. "Richard's liquid holdings amount to three hundred sixty-four million, nine hundred twenty-one thousand, seven hundred fifty-three dollars and twelve cents. His—"

"You just happen to know it down to the cent?"

She shrugged again without taking her gaze off the paintings. "It's my *job* to know down to the penny."

"Is it your job to memorize the figure?"

A wan smile twitched her lips. "His stock portfolio is worth seven hundred ninety-eight million, two hundred twenty-seven thousand twelve dollars and seventy-three cents. But the real money is in the firm."

"Those first two numbers don't count as real money? I need to move to Brooklyn," said Leery.

"The firm pulls in between two-thirds and three-quarters of a billion dollars a year. Richard had fifty-one percent of the stock. Merris holds twenty, and the little sneak holds twenty-nine. So, adding between three hundred thirty-three million and three hundred eighty-two million in annual income to Merris's bottom line in perpetuity amounts to a lot of money."

"Why did he hold so few shares?" asked Dru as she tapped a glossy fingernail on the piano's Pepto-Bismol lacquer.

"You'd have to ask them, but from conversations I had with Richard, Merris doesn't contribute much over the bare minimum. Richard pulled in a lot of the billable hours, and Myercough does the prognostication. Plus, Merris was young and stupid when he and Richard partnered up."

"Interesting," said Leery. "Don't you find it strange he never mentioned all this, Dru?"

She shrugged. "Did Merris know the contents of the Brook will?"

Lena nodded. "Sure he did. He brought the last codicil to me in person. It wasn't sealed."

"Merris brought you Brook's will?"

"It's not so uncommon," she said. "And Richard had called to tell me Merris was on his way over."

"When was this?"

"Two—no, three weeks ago."

"Hmm. Are you sure it was Richard on the phone?" asked Dru.

"I recognized his voice."

"But you and Richard never spoke about the changes to the will?"

"No. He *was* a magister. He knew the proper language as well as I did. I just filed it as he asked."

"Merris is also a magister," said Leery.

"As are many other supernaturals living in New York City. What of it?"

"In addition to being a magister, Merris is a wizard."

"And? I don't understand—"

"You don't? Let me spell it out for you. Wizards cast illusions."

Lena narrowed her eyes. "You think some wizard could fool me?"

"I don't," said Leery. "I think you're in on it."

"In on *what*, Detective?"

"Think about it, Cassidy. You filed a codicil to Richard Brook's will three weeks ago, and I'll bet you a cup of coffee that the will changed the awards set aside for certain beneficiaries." Leery cocked his head and stared at her. "Yours, for instance."

"But I told you, Detective. Richard and I had been talking about our future together. Doesn't it seem likely that he'd want me in his will?"

"You said you and Richard had been talking..." mused Dru. "Was any of it in person?"

"Well, no. Our schedules—"

"Come on, Lena! You live half a block from each other."

She shook her head. "Only on the weekends. Richard spent most of his time at the Sheffield."

"Even though he wanted to marry you?"

She pulled her head back and frowned at him, eyebrows knotted together. "What are you saying?"

"We'll need to examine the codicil," said Dru. "And something you saw Mr. Brook sign with your own eyes."

"I..." She shook her head and drained her glass. "Samuel! Fetch me a copy of Mr. Brook's most recent codicil. Also, bring me a copy of his retainer agreement."

"Not copies," said Dru. "We need the original signatures."

"Fine. Samuel, bring the originals." Lena walked to the bar and made another of her horrible-looking potions. Samuel entered the room a moment later with a leather portfolio, which he handed to her.

Lena lay the portfolio on the piano and flipped it open, arranging the codicil on the right and the retainer agreement on the left, then stepped back and waved Dru and Leery forward.

"Hmm," said Leery. "I'm no expert, but those signatures look exactly alike."

Dru bent and lowered her head closer to the document. She sniffed the paper, ran her fingers over it, then straightened and began making runes in charcoal gray, then connected them with blazing crimson lines. She slapped the rune set on the signature of the codicil and stepped back.

The signature wavered, then smeared as though the ink were still wet and she'd rubbed it with her thumb. Then the inkblot faded and what was left didn't look anything like the signature on the retainer agreement.

"Illusion," Dru said. "And the delivery boy is a wizard."

"A wizard..." Lena took an unsteady step and crumpled into a chair, slopping her crazy drink onto her skirt and the carpet. Her face blanched, and for once, her self-assured mask slipped away. "I..." She shook her head. "I didn't know. The phone calls..." She squeezed her eyes shut.

"I think we need to speak to Harland Merris," said Dru. "It seems he's not who he claims to be."

"Cute joke, Dru," said Leery. "Ms. Cassidy needs to take a ride with us."

"What? I didn't have anything to do with this!"

"That may be true," said Leery. "But we need a formal statement, either way."

18

After dropping Lena Cassidy at the Two-Seven, Dru and Leery rolled downtown and parked in front of Brook Tower. They rode the elevator up to the twenty-second floor and stepped out into the lobby. Glisandra smiled at them from behind the reception desk. "Back again?"

"Where is Harland Merris?" asked Dru.

"Mr. Merris is out for the afternoon," the fairy said. "Both he and Mr. Myercough decided to take the afternoon for personal business."

"Did they leave together?"

"No," said Glisandra. "Mr. Merris left first, then Mr. Myercough had a client visit. He left right after."

Leery and Dru exchanged a glance. "They left together? The client and Myercough?"

"Yes, now that you mention it. And it's strange. Mr. Myercough didn't speak to me, but the client did."

"Take us to Myercough's office."

SURE 'LOCK 153

Her eyes snapped open wide, and her mouth made another perfect O, but she turned and led them around the wall that separated the lobby and the rest of the firm. She led them to his office, but it was empty.

Leery spun and pointed at the corner office with tapestries covering the glass walls. "There!" He sprinted across the suite and jerked the door open.

Myercough lay on the floor, trussed up like a holiday turkey, his tie turned into a gag and drawn tight behind his head. The goblin's eyes bulged at them.

Dru rushed to his side and loosened the tie. "Mr. Myer"—she coughed—"are you all right?"

Myercough heaved in a long breath and said, "Untie me." Leery worked the knots at his ankles while Dru undid his hands. The goblin sat up, rubbing his wrists. "Merris—"

"Yes, we guessed as much," said Dru. "He distracted you, incapacitated you, then created a double?"

"He pretended to be a client," said Myercough, nodding. "Then he put me to sleep with one of his infernal dusts." He glanced over Leery's shoulder at Glisandra. "*Who is answering the phones?*" he bellowed, and she disappeared with a squeak.

"Dusts?" asked Leery.

"Merris pretends at being 'only a wizard' but practices other arts. Alchemy, for one."

Dru nodded. "And evocation?"

"I've seen him summon and play with firelings. He'd bounce them from hand to hand, make them cavort on his desk, that kind of thing."

"And you didn't think it was strange for a wizard to summon immature ifrits?" asked Dru.

"Look, Merris has trouble focusing on any one thing. That's why Richard had him locked in at twenty percent, while I got twenty-nine, even though I was the newer partner."

"I see," said Leery. "And you're aware of Richard's will?"

Myercough nodded and got to his feet, stamping the circulation back into his feet. "Yes, Merris goes up to forty percent, but that can't be avoided. I will have sixty, and, of course, those percentages will change when we bring on new partners. Our agreement calls for the dilution of shares on an even split between us."

"Well, that sounds like the old will," said Leery.

"The *old* will?" Myercough fixed him with a brutal stare, complete with flared nostrils. "What are you talking about?"

"There was a codicil filed three weeks ago," said Dru. "Merris hand-delivered it to Lena Cassidy."

Myercough cursed in Ghukliak, stomping his feet as he strutted around the room. "He's *cheating*!" he cried after making a complete circle. "What's it say? What do I get? What does Merris get?"

"Well..." Leery grimaced. "Merris gets all Brook's stock, including his shares in the partnership."

"And me? And me?"

Leery lifted his palms out to the side. "Nothing."

"*I'll sue!*" cried the goblin, followed by another string of Ghukliak, this one sounding even more emphatic than the last. "This is a farce! *A farce!* Richard only left that fool twenty percent out of some twisted feeling of obligation! Because of the woman!"

"Wait, wait, wait," said Leery, putting his hand on the goblin's shoulder. "What's this about a woman?"

"Yes, yes!" snapped Myercough. "It happened before I joined the partnership—

before there *even was* a partnership! In fact, it's why there *is* a partnership at all!"

"Slow down," said Dru. "What happened? When?"

Myercough flapped his hand at her. "Richard took one of his little evenings too far, and the woman died three days later. The mundane hospital called it an unknown wasting sickness. She and Merris were related. Brother and sister, or something. He knew about her thing with Richard. He couldn't let it go. He kept digging and digging for an explanation of what happened that last night. He'd read about essence manipulation in some book or other, and he joined one of the mundane groups that 'study magic.' When he thought he knew enough, he tracked Richard down and watched him. He broke in one night while Richard was mid-spell and tried to cast one of his pathetic mundane 'spells' on him. Richard took pity on him and sponsored him into the Covenancy. He arranged for an apprenticeship with a local wizard, and the rest is history."

Leery whistled. "You didn't think that was relevant in Brook's murder investigation?"

"Merris swore me to secrecy! He..." Vast shook his head.

"He what?"

"He caught me padding hours, okay? Just like Brook, but Merris was lily-white. There was nothing I could leverage against him, but he said if I kept his and Richard's past quiet, he would help me doctor the billing data—and he did."

"Where would he go?" asked Dru. "What sparked him to run before he had the money?"

"No idea, no idea," said Myercough. "Must I spoon feed you the entire case?" He began to pace back and forth. "I must concentrate! I need a strategy to hold up that codicil." He stopped and whirled toward Leery, snapping his fingers at him. "Your report number! I'll need that for my injunction."

"What report?"

"The one outlining how Merris concocted that codicil and perpetrated a fraud on the Court."

"Yeah, you'll have to wait on that."

"This is *time-sensitive!* I have to get my injunction signed before the funds are disbursed or it will be impossible to track it all down."

"Right now, the executor is sitting in our precinct house waiting for us to take her statement. I think you have time."

"Pssh!" hissed the goblin as he began to pace again. As he turned back toward them, he snapped his fingers at them again. "Well? Do you think Merris is going to come back here and turn himself in? *Go catch him!*"

"Yeah, you're welcome for untying you." Leery and Dru turned and left him to his pacing. On the way out, they stopped at the reception desk for Merris's home address.

19

The servitor warrior stood next to their car, bending down to give the illusion that he needed line of sight to see them. "We have the entire building surrounded, Detective Oriscoe. It's best for you and your partner to stay here. We'll signal when we have everything under control."

For once, Dru didn't bristle at the suggestion. She only smiled at the servitor warrior. "Thanks. We'll wait right here."

The servitor nodded, then disappeared. Up the block, a moving truck stood on the left side of the street—directly opposite the home of Harland Merris. On the far side of the moving truck, the therianthropes and servitor warriors of the SWAT unit were staging, lining up behind the Ganeshan breacher.

"Summoning a fireling is one thing," he said in a musing tone.

"Yes, and a Barghest takes significantly more skill and more willpower, but we don't know how long Merris has studied evocation on the sly. But…I've been thinking."

"About what?"

"Gemble-Croix. If his evocation worked, then perhaps Merris didn't need to summon the creature from Gehenna."

"Can you do that? Take over someone else's summoned creature?"

"Based on Gemble-Croix's spell, I'd say anything is possible. And Kasadya did find one Barghest unaccounted for."

"Yeah, I guess you're right." He watched the Ganeshan break and run across the street, leap up the stoop, lower his head, and smash

Harland Merris's front door to toothpicks. The rest of the SWAT unit sprinted inside behind him. "Still, though, I wish we'd heard something on the Barghest Gemble-Croix sicced on the city."

"Don't fret, Leery," said Dru. "Kasadya is a born tracker. He will find the creature soon."

"Sure, sure," said Leery, "but—"

The brownstone belonging to Harland Merris shuddered on its foundation, and a hurricane roar rattled the windows. The buildings on either side shook as though in the grip of a mild earthquake and their ground-floor windows shattered.

"Uh-oh," said Leery.

"Stay in the car, Leery," said Dru, even as she opened her door and leaped out, already forming red and purple runes with each hand.

"I don't think so," murmured Leery. He jumped out of the car and kicked off his shoes, jerking at his tie.

"Leery! Stay out of this!"

He unbuttoned his shirt and unclasped his belt, studiously not looking at his partner. The thundering roar coming from Merris's house increased in pitch and volume as he shoved his trousers down past his knees and began his transformation.

"Leery! No!" cried Dru as she raced forward, a seventeen-pointed set of purple runes connected by silver lines on her left, and twenty-two scarlet runes waiting for the twenty-third and their connecting lines on her right.

Payot sprang from his temples, thick and glossy, and the hair atop his head began to knit itself into his *yarmulke*. The amulet Lucifer had given him shimmered, and his black woolen hat appeared on his head. His fur sprang out of his skin, still patchy in places but thick and healthy everywhere else.

Dru completed her scarlet runes and connected them with lines the color of blood. She stood on the sidewalk between Leery and Merris's brownstone, each hand ready to hurl a rune set.

The top of the building began to crumble around the edges, bricks flying in circles as though in the grip of a tornado. The shutters peeled away from the brick walls and flew in all directions, spinning and slicing the air.

Leery threw back his head and howled at the noise. Dru glanced his way, frowned at him, and opened her mouth to scream at him, but the roaring rose to a fever-pitch, followed by a massive thump, then perfect silence. The ground shook for a moment, then subsided.

"I don't like this," said Dru. She glanced at him crossly. "Get out of here, Leery. Get back in the car!"

Another thud sounded from the bones of the brownstone, and the front wall of the building bowed, then straightened. A servitor warrior appeared next to the car, then looked around wildly, spotted them and flew over. "Fall back!" he clanged in his metallic voice. "Retreat!"

A second servitor warrior formed in the street facing the house, blazing golden light surrounding him. He threw his arms wide at waist height, and a gonging shout rattled the windows up and down the street. He lifted his arms and clapped his hands together in front of him, and a crack appeared in the sidewalk, then widened until the basement wall of Merris's brownstone appeared. The servitor warrior standing near them rushed forward, already chanting incantations and gathering his power. The front wall of the brownstone shook and bowed again, and the servitors moved to the side.

With a thundering crack, the front wall of the building split, puking bricks and timbers into the street. A massive stone foot followed the debris and thudded into the street.

Dru hurled the purple rune set and began another. One of the servitors called down lightning, while the other hurled a fireball the size of a VW Bug at the thing emerging from Merris's building.

The massive foot was followed by a leg of solid granite, then a hand of stone grasped one side of the gaping hole in the front of the building and shoved. That side of the brownstone crumbled to the ground, and through the dust, a pair of amber glowing eyes appeared.

Dru's rune set settled over the massive foot on the sidewalk, and the visible arm and leg shuddered as it dug in. The creature roared, and it sounded like a granite cliff falling into the sea during the worst storm Leery could imagine. The massive stone creature lurched out of the building, leaving destruction in its wake, and hopped on one foot, kicking the other in the air in an attempt to shake off Dru's runes.

"Stone elemental!" Dru cried. She flung the scarlet rune set, and Leery watched it fly toward the creature's huge stone head. The servitor warriors continued to hurl power at the thing, but with almost no visible effect. Dru wiped away the rune set she'd begun a moment before and began a new one the color of lava.

Leery itched to charge, instinct demanding he attack, that he lunge toward the elemental's throat, but his human side knew that for the folly it was. He watched one of the servitors flick a bolt of power into the crack in the sidewalk—the crack that was now between the elemental's legs—and it blasted the wall of the basement into a thousand pieces. Leery cocked his head, confused.

The other servitor threw his hands toward the sky and shouted in a brassy language Leery couldn't understand. The sky split with too many lightning bolts to count, and thunder rolled from horizon to horizon. The bolts slammed to earth all around the elemental, but none of them hit the stone behemoth.

A werewolf howled somewhere inside Merris's home—a howl of confusion and desperation—and Leery threw his own voice toward the heavens in answer. He darted forward, his wolf side unwilling to let the young werewolf's call for help go unanswered. They were Pack, after all.

"Leery! No!" cried Dru.

The stone elemental turned its head down toward the servitor warriors casting spell after spell against it. It opened its mouth and issued a basso roar that bordered on the unbearable yet inaudible. Moving with impossible quickness, the behemoth slammed its fist down, hammering one of the servitors into the pavement. The other stood its ground, calling for fire and sheathing the elemental's head with it.

Leery bolted between the creature's legs and leaped into the crack in the sidewalk. At the bottom of the crevice, the wall gaped, blackness beckoning. Without pausing, he dashed into the darkness, howling as he went.

"Leery!" Dru screamed. She turned to the elaborate rune set she was creating and began lacing lines of fire between the existing runes with her left hand while adding yet more runes with her right.

The servitor warrior crushed into the asphalt reappeared on top of the moving van and shot lightning from its fingertips into the elemental's face. The behemoth gaped at him, then rushed across the street with both hands extended as though it wanted to grab the servitor and give him a hug. As it reached the center of the road, the servitor atop the moving truck threw his hands out toward the street and began to chant. He flung his hands toward the sky, and the behemoth looked up.

But it should have looked in the other direction. Lightning poured up from the asphalt, from every scorched mark made by the lightning storm the servitor had called down moments before. The bolts crackled and snapped, weaving around one another in a way that seemed intentional, intelligent.

The servitor warrior on the moving van stood his ground as the stone elemental brought its gaze down from the sky and focused on the truck. He kept chanting, even as the behemoth reached out and wrapped him in its stone fist.

Dru finished the seventy-third rune and connected it, then screeched in the *Lingua Tenebris Lacuna* and flung the enormous rune set with its spider web of connecting lines at the elemental's back.

The servitor warrior in the street added his voice and power to the chant of the other, spreading his arms wide, and more electricity jumped from the earth to join the pillars of sparkling power standing in the roadway. The pillars began to twine and join, forming giant legs, and flickered upward to create a torso, head, and arms. The lightning elemental crackled and sputtered sparks for a moment, then its gaze locked on the servitor warrior in the crushing grip of the stone elemental. "Masssster," it hissed. The stone behemoth slapped its hands together, obliterating the servitor it held, and the lightning elemental shrieked and rushed forward, wrapping limbs of pure energy around the stone figure, arcing bolts of electricity the thickness of a man's thigh into the stone behemoth in a multitude of spots.

Dru's rune set slapped against the side of the stone elemental's head, knocking it to the side and burning into the stone like a jet of raw magma from the heart of a volcano. The massive boulder that formed the stone elemental's head began to glow, char, and crack, and the creature's trunk also glowed a dull orange where the lightning beast's arms and bolts touched it.

The obliterated servitor warrior reappeared standing next to Dru, grinning. "Good idea," he said in his metallic voice. "The lightning elemental will contain it. We've grafted ours to draw more power from—"

The stone elemental loosed its throbbing earthquake roar and spun in the lightning elemental's grasp. Stone fists grabbed electricity, and the behemoth roared again. Lightning arced down from the sky, and thunder rolled again. The servitor's elemental swelled, hulking upward, limbs thickening, growing, spectrum shifting from purple to blue to bluish-white. It pushed the stone behemoth into the moving van, crushing the box beneath the weight of the boulders, and bent it back, back, back, until the massive stone that served as the stone elemental's body splintered and cracked.

"Well done, that," said the servitor. "We've got this, though we thank you for your assistance."

"Where is your team? Where is Merris?" Dru asked.

"Merris summoned the elemental, and we distracted it as it grew in size so that our therianthropes could escape to the basement. In the confusion, Merris was able to complete a blink."

"Teleportation spell?"

"Yes, but one limited in scope. It's good for a few hundred steps at best."

"Then he should be close by." Dru ran toward the crack in the sidewalk. "Leery! Leery, I need that nose of yours!" She dropped into the crevasse and darted through the broken wall into the basement. "Leery!"

A werewolf howled somewhere in the dark.

She followed the sound of it through the dust and gloom. Leery stooped over the Ganehsan, who lay unconscious on the floor, blood gushing from a laceration that spanned the width of his great skull. The Ketuan skin-walker leaned against the wall, cradling an arm with its three others, and the young werewolf member of the team crouched over the Garudan who appeared stunned.

"Merris is getting away." Dru put a hand on Leery's shoulder and pushed him away from the Ganeshan, already spinning blue runes with her other hand. "Take the other wolf and track him. He can teleport short distances, so you may lose the scent from time to time. He probably blinked out the back wall of this building, so you'll have to circle the block."

Leery let her move him out of the way, then he barked at the young wolf. He turned and picked his way out of the basement. When they reached the cracked sidewalk, they watched the stone behemoth thrash in the grip of the lightning elemental for a few moments and then broke into a run for the corner. Behind him, the young wolf whined, and Leery barked encouragement.

They circled around the block, racing up the street toward the building that shared a back wall with Merris's place. Leery lifted his snout as he ran to the brownstone, tasting the scents on the wind, comparing them to the odor the magister had given off at the firm. The scent was there, though different, mustier, dustier.

Howling his victory, Leery chased the scent to the end of the block, then lost it. He slid to a stop, nose up, then twisted in a full circle. The SWAT werewolf growled and pointed kitty-corner across the intersection. He dashed diagonally across the intersection, ignoring the blasting horns of the cars that missed him by a whisker.

On the opposite corner, the werewolf howled and pointed down the block. Leery waited for a bread truck to rumble past, then sprinted across the street. As he did, something flashed in the tail of his eye.

Harland Merris, appearing on the corner the young wolf had just vacated. He darted a look over his shoulder at the werewolf, then turned onto the side street and began to walk away at a casual pace.

Leery snarled to himself, then ran through the crosswalk. He caught up with the magister after a few long, loping strides, launching himself at Merris's back at the last second. He howled as he struck the magister, and the SWAT wolf howled back. Leery and Merris tumbled on the sidewalk, a ball of snarling fur and human skin that glittered with enchanted power. He had his arms and legs wrapped around Merris by the time they slowed to a halt, his fangs brushing the back of the magister's neck.

"*Ictu!*" cried Merris, and Leery was left on the sidewalk, arms empty.

Leery growled in frustration and whirled to his feet, his gaze zipping around to locate Merris, but he needn't have bothered. The SWAT wolf had him pinned to the sidewalk fifty paces back toward Merris's street, one clawed hand covering the magister's mouth, teeth bared.

Leery threw back his head and howled, long and loud, then rushed to the young wolf's side.

After a few moments, a horrendous crash sounded from the direction of Merris's brownstone, and a servitor warrior popped into existence a few hundred yards down the street.

"Good work!" he called, then disappeared and reappeared next to them. He chanted "*Silentium*!" and pointed at Merris. He cast another spell to bind the magister's hands and feet, then nodded at Leery and clapped the SWAT wolf on the back. "Your partner has stabilized the injured," he said. "Good work, David."

The SWAT wolf yipped and wagged his long tail.

20

Epatha Van Helsing floated into the observation room, a wide smile on her translucent face. "Nice to see you can wade into a batty-fang without ending up grinning at the daisy roots," she said to Leery.

"Hey, one time, Lieu. One time I got myself killed."

"For most of us, it only takes the one," she said with a girlish giggle.

"It pays to have friends." Leery jutted his chin toward the one-way glass.

"Does she have our friend on the whisper yet?"

"No, but give her a minute."

"Better get in there and play her Adam. See if you can make it two in a row without dancing upon nothing."

"One time, Lieu," said Leery, his hand on the doorknob. "And it was justified."

"Yes, it was, but you could let a girl tease you about it for as much lally-gagging as you get about. Now, get in there."

Leery grinned and twisted the doorknob. "Hey there, Counselor," he said in a jovial tone. "Glad to see you."

Lena Cassidy grimaced and hung her head.

"Looks like you've gotten yourself into quite a mess. Or is that expression on your face just the hangover from your bartending skills?"

"I didn't do anything wrong," she said peevishly. "I thought I was doing what Richard wanted. I'm a victim, here, too."

"That remains to be seen," said Dru.

"You know what we didn't find with Harland Merris?" asked Leery as he circled around behind Cassidy, tapping the back of her chair as he went.

"How could I know?"

"We didn't find anything about summoning a Barghest. Not in any of his books, not in his notes, and not in his secret summoning lab. Then again, the lab is hardly more than rubble at this point."

"So? What does that have to do with how he used illusions to perpetrate fraud on me?"

"This *Maleficium Zenunim*... Did you tell me some practitioners use it to summon lesser incubi, partner?"

One of Dru's eyebrows shot up, and she pursed her lips.

"It doesn't matter if the princess backs your pathetic lie, wolfman. *I* didn't summon a Barghest and sic it on Richard."

"Do you think Kasadya will tell us the same thing?"

Cassidy blanched at the demon's name but nodded. "He will."

"So, tell us how it was supposed to work," said Dru. "Obviously, Richard had to die, but you never would have countenanced wasting him in a dog run in DeWitt Clinton Park."

"I would never have countenanced his murder, no matter the method."

"Yeah, I get why you would say that…*now*, but Harland Merris paints a different picture."

"*Lies*," hissed Lena. "Whatever he says about me, it's a lie! He-he-he *duped* me!"

Leery glanced at Dru and raised an eyebrow. She lifted one shoulder, then turned her gaze back to Cassidy. "Say we believe you that you wouldn't have played along with a murder. How was the codicil supposed to play out? Obviously, had he lived, Richard would have found out about the fake, and then neither you nor Merris would have seen a dime."

"I would have *gladly* shown the codicil to Richard. If he then said it was a fake, I would have been the first to phone the police and report it."

"Hmm." Leery took a seat beside Dru. "I know Dru already asked this, but are you sure you don't want representation?"

"I'm a magister, Detective."

"Yeah, I know that, but—"

"I don't need a defense magister to help me avoid landmines. There aren't any. I have only the truth to tell you, and it will be the same story no matter when you ask your questions, and no matter who is in the room."

Dru leaned forward and rested her forearms on the table, hands clasped. "You had no inkling that the codicil was anything other than genuine?"

"No. None." Tears brimmed in her eyes. "I... At first—with the phone calls, you know—I wondered about Richard's change of heart. He'd seemed so vehement when we broke up..." She shook her head and dashed the tears from her eyes. "I... I told myself they were words spoken in haste, and that the intervening time had..." She dropped her gaze to her lap. "Merris played me exactly right," she murmured. "He told me what I wanted most in the world to believe."

"Hey, maybe it *was* Richard on the other end of those phone calls," said Leery.

But Lena shook her head. "No. I guess part of me always knew it was too good to be true."

"One question, though," said Dru. "If Merris was in it for the money, why would he give all that cash to you? He didn't need to. He could have given you a part of it or something less valuable, like the Sheffield flat."

Lena nodded without lifting her gaze. "I think he wasn't sure I was buying it. He kept insisting he loved me, that he wanted to marry me, even after I said I would marry him. It was as though he couldn't take yes for an answer." She lifted her face and stared at Dru. "I think the money was because he thought I suspected him. That if I was getting something material out of it, I wouldn't question the other changes too deeply."

"Okay," said Leery, resting his hands on his knees and leaning forward. "That's all I've got for you, Ms. Cassidy, so unless Dru has something..." He glanced at her, and Dru shook her head.

"Then let me go speak with our lieutenant, and we'll see what's what." He stood and crossed into the observation room. He moved to Van Helsing's side and stared through the one-way glass as she was. "What do you think, Lieu?"

Van Helsing shrugged. "I'm not sure, but we don't have any evidence that she was anything more than what she claims."

"Only the admission of *Maleficium Zenunim* practice. She wraps men up and feeds on them on a routine basis."

"Her license checks out on that front. I think we'll believe her about Merris duping her. For now. We can always arrest Ms. Cassidy later."

"You're the boss, Boss."

"You got that right, Oriscoe. Kick her loose. I'll go call Angie and let her know."

Chapter 3

The Court Case

I

Angie closed the folder containing the police report on Harland Merris. She crossed her arms and slouched back in the chair, staring down at the folder.

"Well?" asked Sam.

"Something feels..."

"Yeah, that's what I think," said Sam. "Has the demon tracker found the Barghest?"

Angie shook her head. "Nothing yet. It's as if the thing showed up to kill Brook and then disappeared into the mist. There have been no more sightings. No reports other than the original witness."

"But we know the Barghest has not returned to Gehenna? It wasn't one of the licensed evocations?"

"That's correct," said Angie wearing a grim expression.

"And the other partner in the firm? The...sorcerer?"

"The *goblin* sorcerer?" she asked with a wisp of a smile. "Oh, he's raving mad, demanding we release our injunction on disbursing the proceeds of the will and let probate proceed."

"Remind me never to partner with a goblin."

"Somehow, I don't think that will be an issue." Angie grinned and tilted her head to the side, letting her luxurious black hair slide over her shoulder. "Can you imagine a goblin LM?"

"No." He leaned forward and tapped the police report. "What do we do? Proceed?"

"Isn't it your job to tell me that? *Boss*."

Sam smiled sourly. "Yeah. I get all the fun."

"Don't forget the big bucks."

"Right. The *big* bucks." He grinned across the desk. "At least no one will murder me for their inheritance."

2

Angie stood in her accustomed spot, waiting for the judge to arrive and arraign Harland Merris. He sat on the prisoner's bench, looking around as though he'd never seen the inside of a courtroom before. Every time she glanced in his direction, he tried to signal her, tried to hiss at her.

King Arthur floated into the courtroom, perfect as always in his gleaming armor, hand resting on the massive stone set in Excalibur's hilt. He came to the center of the courtroom and gazed out at the gallery. He cleared his throat, then spoke in a mellow baritone. "Her Honor, Judge Morgana Le Fey, is feeling out of sorts at her out-of-turn assignment to the arraignment. I'd advise those present with business before the Court to behave, lest you earn her wrath." That said, he floated to the side and called, "All rise!"

Judge Morgana Le Fay zipped through the wall into the courtroom, balls of emerald lightning sparking from her like her own personal light show. She took the bench and frowned at her gavel as it jerked into the air and slammed down on the sound block like a smith's hammer on an anvil. "Let's get this over with," she said. "Who's first?"

"The People vs. Harland Merris, Your Honor," said Angie.

King Arthur floated to Merris and waved him toward the defense table.

"And who stands for the defense?" Le Fay's hostile gaze scanned the gallery. "Who represents this man?"

No one spoke, and no one stood up. Merris turned and scanned the crowd, then glanced at Angie. "Psst! He's not here," he whispered.

"Who is not here, sir?" asked Le Fay in a sickly-sweet voice.

"My partner... My, uh, magister, Your Honor."

"His name?" she asked.

"Vastalan Myer—" he coughed.

"Bless you. Is Mr. Myer in the hall?" A bailiff in the back squeezed out the doors into the hall.

"Excuse me, Judge Le Fay. His name is Myer—" He covered his mouth and coughed.

"Myercough?"

"He's a goblin, Your Honor, and—"

"I don't care if he's the former Grand Cynosure himself. What is his legal name?"

The doors banged open, and a disheveled goblin stood there panting. "My...apologies...Your...Honor. Vastalan Myer"—he coughed without covering his mouth—"for the defense, if it pleases the Court."

"No, it does not. This is a court of law, sir, not a circus, not a theater stage. You need a proper name to argue before me."

"But, Judge Le Fay, that *is* my proper name."

"Not in this courtroom. Here, you are Myercough, or you can find someone else to stand for your client."

"Fine!" snapped Myercough. "Though I object to your bigotry."

Le Fay raised her eyebrow, and King Arthur's ghostly hand slapped down on—and through—Myercough's shoulder. "*Bigotry*, sir?"

"Vastalan Myer*cough* for the defense, Your Honor."

Morgana smiled and tilted her head a little. "Oh, no, sir. I wouldn't want *bigotry* to stand in this courtroom. Let's return to that accusation, shall we?"

The goblin glanced at Arthur and whined, "Forgive me, Your Honor, it appears I misspoke."

"Well, it happens to the best of us. Take your place."

Arthur lifted his hand, and Myercough pushed through the swinging gates in the bar and stood next to Merris, giving him a glare for good measure.

"The People on bail, Ms. Carmichael?"

"We request remand, Your Honor, and request you invoke the Special Treatment Provision of the Canon and Covenants and order the accused to be held in a warded antimagic field to prevent him summoning creatures to aid in his escape."

Le Fay glanced at Merris. "The accused is a warlock?"

"We aren't sure what he is, Your Honor. Only that he has not limited himself to one field of magic, and that he has summoned a Barghest and a stone elemental that we know of."

Morgana lifted her eyebrows. "Why start small?" she murmured. "Mr. Myer*cough*? What does the defense have to add?"

"My client, Your Honor, is an upstanding member of the community, with strong ties in the city. He is a partner in the firm of Brook, Merris, and Myer"—he opened his mouth but snapped it shut at Le Fay's narrowed eyelids—"uh, Myercough, Your Honor. He owns property, he—"

"Property his pet stone elemental all but destroyed."

"—has notable friends on Wall Street and in City Hall. Your Honor, we request you set a reasonable bail."

"Hmm. What's reasonable for a man who summons such uncontrollable terrors in the city limits? For a man who destroys his own property, either through lack of caring or by incompetence?" She gazed up at the ceiling, then looked at Angie. "The Special Treatment Provision is generally applied to dungeon sentences."

"Yes, Your Honor, but it isn't limited to them. In fact, there is no language in the Canon and Covenants describing any limitation of the provision."

Le Fay nodded. "The accused is remanded and ordered held in a warded field of antimagic. Trial date to be set at the earliest convenience of the courts." She flicked her fingers at her gavel, and it banged on the sound block. "Next case!"

3

Leery slept near the fire, his tail curled around his paws, an empty, blood-splattered tray lying next to him. Dru gazed at him fondly, sipping her bowl of blood.

"He barely even looked at you when you took the bowl tonight, dearest," said Agrat.

"Yes."

"Wise of him," said Hercule with a laugh in his voice.

Dru grinned. "Yes."

Lucifer shifted, and his big chair creaked beneath him. "He's healing well. He should be back to full strength in a matter of weeks. Things will get back to normal for him."

Dru lost her grin. "Yes."

"His daughter asks many questions," said Hercule.

"And you're answering them?"

"*Mais bien sûr.* It is what Leery asked of me."

"Yes," said Dru. "Do you think your answers are…"

"Dissuading her?" Hercule sighed. "The wisdom of old age is wasted on the young. She has perhaps lost some of her more romantic notions of unlife, but she sees what her father has become, and...I find it hard to argue against that."

"Besides," said Agrat. "Children grow up and go their own way."

Dru could hear the smile in her voice and pursed her lips to keep from joining her mother.

4

The fire had burned down to embers by the time Leery awoke. He'd changed back in his sleep and found the floor cold, hard. He straightened and looked around. Three empty normal-sized chairs sat behind him in the dark, as did the Prince of Darkness, himself, in his giant chair. "Oh, hello, Luci," said Leery.

"Leery," said Lucifer. "Did you sleep well?"

"I always do after my wolf eats."

"Your strength is returning. Soon, you will be able to return to your home."

Leery grinned as he dressed. "Tired of me already?"

"Not at all, my friend. But it wasn't my feelings I was thinking of."

"Oh," said Leery, looking at the ground. "Yeah, I get it."

"She's special to me." Lucifer rolled his boulder-shoulders in a shrug.

"Me, too, Luci." He shrugged his shirt over his head, still half-buttoned. "But…"

"This partner thing."

"Yes." Leery grabbed his shoes and socks and sat in the normal-sized chair next to Lucifer.

"Maybe the other thing is more important than the partner thing."

"Maybe," said Leery, "but Dru and I are at opposite ends of our careers. She's just starting, and I'm"—he flashed a sour smile—"well-worn."

"Perhaps Dru feels differently?"

"We *have* talked about it, you know."

"I do know. But perhaps it's time to talk about it again."

Leery nodded. "Has she said something?"

"No, but the time you've both spent here—her caring for you, you two always together—she regrets that it's about to end."

Oriscoe frowned. "I hadn't thought about that yet. She's got that big place she rolls around in by herself. I've just got that little—"

"Are you sure your little cracker box won't feel empty without her?"

Leery looked at the remains of the fire. "Maybe it will."

"These rules your police department has... They don't extend to my domain, Leery."

"I know. But it's not just the rules, Luci. She already worries too much about me."

"And you do the same, Leery. Unless you always attack dragons while already half-dead."

"That's different. I made promises—to you, to Hercule, to Agrat, even to Gregory."

Lucifer's lips curled into a smile. "Ah. And without those promises, you would have let Agon do what he wanted?"

"Well...no, but that's not—"

"Yes, it *is* the same thing." Luci leaned forward and rested a big hand on Leery's shoulder. "You know it, I know it, and Dru knows it."

Leery took a deep breath and puffed out his cheeks. "So, what? We get married and have little werewolf-vampires?"

"That's up to you two."

Leery glanced at the Tempter over his shoulder. "You know one thing those Bible stories got right about you?"

Lucifer frowned. "What's that?"

"You really know how to tempt a guy."

Luci chuckled. "But this time, it's not me doing the tempting. It's Dru."

"Oh, sure, blame the cute succubus."

A soft knock came at the door. "Come in, Angie," called Lucifer. "I'm just—"

"Your pardon, Lord," said a matte black figure standing in the hall. "Kasadya has found the Barghest."

5

The Barghest circled the Lake in Central Park, one nose to the ground as though tracking a scent, the other head scanning the trees surrounding it. It left a trail of diaphanous black smoke in its wake and the orangish fire in its pelt reflected from the surface of the water. It seemed to be walking without any destination in mind.

Dru wrote mercury runes in the air beside her, and Leery kept watch on the beast. "Are you sure this will work?" he asked.

"Yep," said Dru. "I played with these guys as a girl. They're big babies, really."

"I'll take your word for it."

"The only danger will be if it decides to go traipsing through a part of the park with a higher headcount."

"How do we keep it from doing that?"

"That's what these runes are for, silly," she said and bumped him with her shoulder. "I'm sending him home via Uncle Luci's instructions."

"Good. Hey, these things don't *breathe* fire, do they?"

"What, like a dragon? Don't be silly. Think of them as the pet Gregory would have if he could be bothered."

"Oh."

"Almost done. Quit worrying."

Dru added another rune to her set, then connected them with burnished gold. "There. That should do it." She tapped the top rune and pushed the diagram over on its side and spun it. She spoke a few lines in the *Verba*

Patiendi, then flicked the rune set toward the Barghest.

They watched it circle above the beast like a UFO, then as it darted down to lay on the Barghest's back, the two-headed creature snarled and juked to the side, then faced them and snarled.

"Crap!" Dru said rapidly sketching more runes. "It must have seen it in the water."

"Should I change?" Leery asked, slipping one foot out of his shoe.

"If you want to get into a war for dominance, sure."

"Then what?"

"I'll have this rune set cast in a second. Whatever you do, don't look it in the eye."

"Because it will steal my soul?"

"Because it will take it as a challenge and attack you. Remind me to talk to you about your superstitions."

"Right." He tried to look at the Barghest without looking at it and had to give up. "Tell me what you want me to do."

Dru sighed. "Well, it looks like I want you to run, now."

"What?" His gaze darted toward where the Barghest had been, only to find the beast halfway across the park, leaving charred paw prints in the grass and booking it for Central Park West. "Le sigh," he said and started running. He grabbed his handheld radio. "Vinny? He's on the move, heading west."

The Barghest darted through the late-night traffic like a professional running back cutting through linebackers, then darted up West 75th Street. Dru spun a slate gray rune set into existence and flung it at the retreating beast, but like with the first spell, the Barghest sensed the tracer spell and dodged with uncanny grace.

"That's not fair!" Leery shouted. "Take your runes like a good doggy."

The Barghest glanced back with one head, fiery eyes sparkling, while the other kept track of where it was going. Its tongue lolled and fire dripped from it.

"I really hate fire," said Leery.

"Stay back this time," said Dru. "He won't attack me."

"You sure about that?"

"I'm his princess."

The Barghest cut to the right close to the end of the block, its triangular orange claws digging furrows in the asphalt, and it darted down a flight of steps into a dark alley. Dru and Leery followed it, barely slowing enough not to fall down the steps.

At the bottom of the stairs, everything was black and silent. Dru stepped forward, her blood garnet-jeweled staff out in front giving off a hot red light.

"Careful," said Leery. "I can't hear it moving anymore."

"Relax, Leery. I know these creatures—"

A blood-curdling snarl cut her off and then the Barghest was on her, two sets of jaws snapping, four eyes blazing hellfire, flame dripping from its coat like water. Dru got her staff up sideways between them. The Barghest outweighed her by at least two hundred pounds, and its momentum carried her over backward onto the ground.

Leery let his wolf out in one seam popping, leather-snapping moment and dove at the beast, his own jaws wide but having no idea *which* neck to clamp between them. He bowled the Barghest off Dru and together they rolled in the trash littering the alley—a mass of snapping teeth and sweeping talons and fire.

A whistle as loud as one of the Seven Trumpets blasted through the alley, and everyone froze for a heartbeat. In that moment, a ball of brilliant white light bounced past them, Leery and Dru's gaze locked on it.

"Go get it, boy," said Vinny Gonofrio.

Yipping, the Barghest turned and ran after the glowing ball, its tail wagging from side to side with enough vigor to pull its whole back end back and forth with it. It leaped and attacked the ball mid-bounce, then turned and ran back to Vinny, tail still going.

"Who's a good boy?" asked Vinny in the special voice grown men reserve for talking to dogs. "You just want to play, don't you?" He held out his hand, and the hound dropped the ball in it, then sat, ears perked, tail swooshing across the alley's bricks. Vinny threw the ball again, and the Barghest darted after it. "You two can get up. Get ready, Princess."

Leery sprang to his feet and offered Dru his paw, then pulled her up. She took a moment to brush the nastiness from her skirt, then sighed and gave up. She began to draw the mercury rune set again. "He can sense my spells," she said.

Vinny nodded. "It's okay. I'll keep him distracted." The Barghest came running back, and Gonofrio crooned at it, took the ball, and held it up. The hound sat, its four-eyed gaze

SURE 'LOCK 199

intent on the glowing ball. "Now would be good."

She completed her runes and connected them with burnished gold lines, then flicked the whole set on its side. This time, she spoke her activation in the *Lingua Tenebris Lacuna*. As the spidery language flared to life in the tepid alley, the Barghest growled and darted a gaze toward her.

"Hey, now, it's okay," said Vinny. "Who's my good boy? You want this ball, boy? You want to keep this?"

The hound turned its full attention back to Gonofrio, and Dru flicked the rune set into the air above it. As it descended around him, Vinny held out the ball, and with ginger slowness, the Barghest opened one set of jaws and took it. With the other mouth, it yipped.

"Aw, you're welcome. I wish I could play with you more, but you're needed at home."

The silver rune set encapsulated the Barghest, then it grew smaller and smaller until it popped out of existence. Vinny glanced at Leery and said, "Are you insane? Barghest take pack dominance seriously, Leery."

Leery transformed. "Hey, it was that or watch him mess up Dru's make up."

"He was just playing," said Vinny.

"If you say so."

"He's back with his littermates, so all's well that ends well, I guess." Gonofrio looked longingly at the spot where the beast had sat. "I love puppies."

6

Judge Samuel Sewall's wooden-faced bailiff thumped the butt of his spear on the marble tiles surrounding the bench. He glared about the courtroom with such fire in his gaze that few returned it. "All rise! The Honorable and Just Samuel Sewall presides over this court! Rise and pay your respects!" Then he banged his spear one final time, and before the echo faded, Samuel Sewall appeared, already seated behind the bench, his hand resting on his gavel. He swept it up and banged it on the sound block, then glared around the courtroom. "I declare this examination of fact in session! You may regain your—"

"Uh, Judge Sewall?"

The bailiff snapped his spear against the floor. "You *dare*, sir?"

Sewall's cold gaze went first to the prosecution table, but both Sam and Angie were staring at the defense. The judge turned to glare at the defense table, behind which sat only Harland Merris. "It is considered most rude to interrupt one's elders, young man."

"I apologize, Your Honor. It's just that my magister isn't here."

"Does your magister think so little of the Court?"

"No, Judge, but we were told Judge Cayce would be presiding over the trial. It may be that—"

The gallery doors burst open, and all eyes turned to the back of the room. Vastalan Myercough stood in the doorway, panting and wiping sweat from his brow. "Your...Honor...I...apologize." He leaned against the jamb. "I've just run from Judge Cayce's courtroom, where I have been waiting since—"

"I expect magisters operating in my courtroom to be punctual, Mister..."

"Myer"—he coughed without covering his mouth—"Your Honor. But I'm only here to beg the Court's indulgence. I have a motion here requesting permission to withdraw from this case."

"Most unusual. Most unusual," Sewall muttered. "Bring it here, if you must." He pointed at a spot on the bench and stared at it while Myercough made his way through the bar and set the blueback before him. Sewall scanned the document and grimaced. "Is this true, sir?" He lifted a steely-eyed gaze to Myercough's face.

"Yes, Your Honor, every word."

Sewall grimaced and beckoned Sam. "Sidebar, Counselors."

Sam came to the bench, one eyebrow quirked.

"Mr. Myercough here asserts he is a magister admitted to the bar but not one familiar with criminal law. He states he acted in the arraignment as a favor to his former partner, the defendant, but now he finds his lack of experience troubling."

"Plus, certain information has come my way that makes it impossible for me to represent Merris zealously," said Myercough.

"What do you think, Mr. McCoy."

Sam shrugged. "Your Honor, Mr. Myercough was a potential victim of the fraud perpetrated by the defendant."

"I see, I see," said Sewall. "Motion granted. You may leave the courtroom, sir."

"Thank you, Your Honor," said Myercough. As he turned, he sneered at Merris, then blew by the defense table and out the door.

Merris looked as though a stiff wind might end him.

"I take it the defendant did not know of the motion?"

Merris shook his head.

"Have you another magister?"

"I am a magister, Your Honor."

"Are you saying you wish to proceed *pro se*?"

Merris shook his head. "Definitely not, Your Honor."

"I see." He turned his head to the bailiff. "Head out into the hall. Grab the first supernatural defender you see and bring him before me." The wooden-faced bailiff gave a stiff nod and trotted out to the hall. "This is most unusual," groused Sewall, staring down at Merris as though it were all his fault. The door at the back of the room banged open, and the bailiff pulled Geoffrey Laveau into the room bodily. "Ah! Mr. Laveau. Meet your client...uh..."

"Harland Merris," said McCoy.

"Quite right. Mr. Laveau, meet your new client, Harland Merris. Mr. Merris, may I present Mr. Geoffrey Laveau, supernatural defender."

"Your Honor? This is not my client," said Laveau.

Sewall smiled at him—a shark considering his dinner. "That's where you are mistaken, Mr. Laveau."

"But I have a full caseload already, Your—"

"And now you have one more." Sewall dismissed him with a wave of his gavel. "Take your place, Magister."

The bailiff kept his hand on Laveau's arm until they reached the defense table as though afraid the magister might turn and bolt. Laveau glanced at McCoy hopelessly.

"Good. Now, we are ready to proceed."

"But, Your Honor! I don't even know the particulars of the case!"

"Then Mr. McCoy's opening statement should be quite informative."

"Your Honor, I move for permission to withdraw—"

"Not on your life, Counselor," said Sewell.

"In that case, Judge Sewall, I must insist on a continuance to prepare my case."

"Insist, must you?" growled Sewall, narrowing his eyes at the young magister. Laveau stood his ground, not cutting his eyes away, and Sewall sighed. "Objections, Mr. McCoy?"

"As long as this doesn't impact our speed clock, Your Honor, the People don't object to a short continuance."

Sewall puffed out his cheeks. "One day, Mr. Laveau. Not one second more."

"Thank you, Your Honor, but one day—"

"Sir, your client is a magister. He can help you get up to speed. He is intimate with the details of the case, after all." Sewall slammed his gavel on the sound block and disappeared, letting the gavel clatter to the bench.

7

Later that afternoon, as Sam and Angie sat in his office discussing another case, Geoffrey Laveau knocked on the door.

Sam waved him in, his face set in a sour grimace. "What do you want, Laveau?"

"Let's talk, Mr. McCoy. Ms. Carmichael, it's pleasant to see you again."

Angie forced a smile on her face.

Sam spread his hands. "What do we have to talk about?"

"Harland Merris." He came into the office and sat across the table from Angie. "He's willing to testify to reduce his sentence, and not to put too fine a point on it, but it would help me a lot to plead this out."

Sam shook his head a little and glanced at Angie. "It's your nickel, sir."

"Testify against who?" asked Angie. "By all accounts, Harland Merris was the lone actor here."

Laveau shook his head. "He merely drew up the paperwork and delivered it to the executor of the will. Your own investigators have already interviewed another accomplice and the mastermind behind the plot."

Sam raised his craggy eyebrows. "And who would these mysterious accomplices be? Mr. Myercough, I bet?"

"First, let's talk deal."

"No, Mr. Laveau. Without details, I have no deal to offer your client."

"Lena Cassidy is the accomplice. The mastermind is a warlock named...I have it here somewhere..." Laveau pinched the bridge of his nose, then turned, and in a flurry of loose papers, he dug out his notes. "Ah. Bevin Gemble-Croix."

Angie shook her head. "The police investigated both of those individuals, Laveau. Gemble-Croix is guilty of being a twit seventy-eight years ago, but I'm afraid the statute of limitations has expired on that crime. Your client hoodwinked Lena Cassidy. She's on our witness list, as you will see when you get around to preparing your case."

Laveau's shoulders slumped. "Mr. McCoy, *help* me. My client says he acted on Gemble-Croix's instructions. Something to do with an initiation in some temple or club, I don't know. He says both he and Cassidy were to split the monies from the victim's will as recompense for the risks they took."

"We'll need more than his word on it, Mr. Laveau," said Sam. "Present his version as an alternate theory of the crime, if you genuinely believe him."

"But—"

"No, Mr. Laveau," Sam said gently. "Our answer—at this time—is no. We can revisit this later, should our position change."

Laveau nodded. "Thanks for your time," he mumbled. He stood and left the office.

"I almost feel sorry for the guy."

"Don't you remember the shenanigans he tried to pull in the fetch trial?"

"I did say *almost*," Sam said with a grin.

8

The next morning everyone sat in their places when Judge Sewall appeared. "I am glad to see everyone is on time this morning. I declare this examination of fact in session!" He nodded, a grave expression on his ghostly face. "And this time, nothing will stop us from getting to the bottom of the crimes charged. I wish to caution the audience, and the magisters who will argue their cases before me, that I will brook no nonsense during this examination. Nonsense makes me cross, and when I am cross, I sometimes order people pressed with stones. I hope that makes my position clear." He arched an eyebrow at McCoy until Sam and Angie nodded, then shifted his attention to Laveau, who cringed, and Sewall puffed out his cheeks. "What is it, Mr. Laveau?"

"Your Honor, one small question, if it pleases the Court."

"It doesn't but go ahead."

"My docket indicates Judge Cayce should be adjudicating the case."

"That is not a question, sir," said the judge. "But I have one for you. Do I look like Judge Cayce?"

Laveau shook his head. "Not at all, Your Honor."

"Indeed, I do not," said Sewall. "But since your docket reads Cayce, I must be him, no?"

"No, Your Honor."

"Ah. Then a reasoning man might conclude that something has occurred since the docket went out. Perhaps Judge Cayce is indisposed. Or perhaps, due to Judge Sewall's expertise in certain areas, Judge Cayce asked him to step in. Or perhaps yet, I wanted to rule on this case because I despise malefactors who abuse creatures from the other side and asked Judge Cayce to step aside."

"Yes, Your Honor. I see the possibilities, but may I ask which one is true in this case?"

Sewall narrowed his eyes. "Mr. Laveau, are you going to insist on giving me a headache? After my little speech about pressing people with stones and everything?"

"Uh... No, Your Honor, but..." Laveau looked down at his feet.

Sewall leaned forward. "But *what*?"

"Your Honor, it's just that we all know about the trials in Salem, and since this case involves a significant amount of spellcraft, I..." He froze as he raised his gaze and saw Sewall's expression. Then he gulped and dropped his gaze. "I move that Your Honor recuses himself from this trial."

Sewall laughed, but it was far from a pleasant sound. "Denied, Counselor."

"But, Your Honor, I—"

"*Denied.*" Sewall turned to McCoy. "Are the People ready to proceed?"

"We are, Your Honor."

"Then do so." Sewall snapped his gaze back to Laveau and used it to drill holes in the magister's head until he sat down.

Sam stood and came around to stand in front of the jury box, smiling his best benign-uncle smile. "Ladies and gentlemen, welcome and good morning. As you've seen, things occasionally go off the rails here in the Criminal Part, but thanks to the attention of our judges, they are put right in quick time. The case you will hear about is convoluted by its very conception. I don't want you to feel self-conscious if you don't understand some aspect of it. Simply ask the bailiff when court is out of session and we'll do our best to clarify things for you. At the same time, the *motive* for this case is simple. Greed, that age-old sin." Sam shrugged, pursing his lips. "And perhaps envy for good measure. You see, the defendant, Mr. Harland Merris, was a named partner in the firm of Brook, Merris, and Myer"—Sam cupped his mouth and coughed—"a well-known Wall Street firm." When some of the juries chuckled at Myercough's name, Sam smiled. "Yes, it's a strange name to our ears, but the gentleman in question belongs to the goblin race. At any rate, Mr. Merris, being the junior of the three, was jealous of Mr. Brook, the senior named partner in the firm—jealous of his status, his wealth, his homes, even his lifestyle—and undertook a foul plan to usurp Mr. Brook's place in the world. Mr. Merris contrived an elaborate plan that included pretending to be Mr. Brook and rekindling an old flame—simply because that old flame was the magister who managed Mr. Brook's will. That brings us to the charge of impersonation of a magical entity, to wit one Lena Cassidy, a practitioner of the arts." McCoy lifted one finger. "You will hear from her in direct testimony. But the defendant's crimes didn't stop there. You see, he concocted a codicil to the will which granted Mr. Merris all of Mr. Brook's stock holdings and his shares in their firm, thus the count of fraud against the Court. This would have made the defendant the senior partner in the firm by a wide margin." McCoy half-turned and shook his head at the defense table. "At the same time, he set out to interfere with a previously-summoned Barghest from the depths of Gehenna—which brings us to the charge of summoning an other-realm entity without a license—I wish you to know that the Barghest in question was already in this realm, but since the defendant did, in fact, use an evocation to bind the hound to *his* will over the will of the original summoner, the charge fits. And his command to this hound set it on Brook's trail, resulting in Mr. Brook's death.

We know what that means." McCoy nodded to the jury. "One count of magical murder in the first degree. But, again, Mr. Merris did not stop there. No"—McCoy let his head droop, and he shook it sadly—"when the police began to close in on the truth, the defendant impersonated two other people, then summoned another dangerous creature and set it loose in Manhattan—a stone elemental, no less. Luckily for Mr. Merris, none of the police officers took significant injury when he commanded his summoned pet to attack them. So, the people add two additional counts of impersonation of a magical entity, and another count of summoning an other-realm entity without a license." Sam turned, gave another glance to the defense, shook his head, and returned to the prosecution table. "Now, I have no doubt that my colleague, Mr. Laveau of the Supernatural Defender's Office, will present an alternate theory of the crime. His version will no doubt cast Mr. Merris as a worker bee or an unwitting accomplice in an attempt to divert your attention to the facts in this case. I don't blame him for it—far from it—as it's his job to provide a zealous defense of Mr. Merris. But I urge you, ladies and gentlemen of the jury, not to be swayed by innuendo and insinuation. Stick to the facts. Stick to verifiable *facts*—that which can be *proven*." He reached his seat and smiled at the jury. "Thank you for your attention." He took his seat and nodded to Judge Sewall.

"Very well. Mr. Laveau? Are you ready to present your opening statement?"

"Yes, Your Honor, and thank you." Laveau stood but didn't move from his spot. "As you know, ladies and gentlemen, I came to this case late and have had extraordinarily little time to prepare my case. So, I will be playing catch up to Mr. McCoy, and if I'm honest, I'll admit Mr. McCoy is at least twice the magister I am. He has more experience—by far—and, I'll warrant, a better grasp of the statutes. I'd be playing catch up no matter how much time I had to prepare." He smiled at the jury and met each person's gaze before he went on. "Now, humility aside, I take issue with some of the things Mr. McCoy has told you. For one, if I present something to you, *it will be provable*, not innuendo, not insinuation. For another, there is an alternate theory of the crime, and the prosecutor knows what it is. You see, I met with Mr. McCoy and Ms. Carmichael yesterday to convey my client's willingness to testify against the real mastermind behind these crimes. Unfortunately for my client, Mr. McCoy is a bird-in-the-hand kind of prosecutor, and he declined the offer." Laveau held up his hand like a crossing guard commanding traffic to stop. "But don't worry. As Mr. McCoy has asserted, I will be presenting this information to you as part of my client's defense. Rest assured; you will have all the information you need to decide this matter." He began to sit but then surged upward. "Oh, and one more thing. I had a wily old professor who once told me that if a case is too complex to easily understand, you haven't reached the bottom of it, yet. Please bear that in mind." He gave the jury a small bow. "Thank you, that's all I have."

"Very well," said Sewall. "Mr. McCoy, call your first witness."

"My pleasure, Your Honor. I call Detective Leery Oriscoe to the stand."

The wooden-faced bailiff fetched Leery, swore him in, and led him to the witness box. Leery sat and grinned at the jury. "Hello, folks," he said. "I would've brought coffee but the mean bailiff wouldn't let me."

"Good morning, Detective Oriscoe," said Sam with a small grin on his face. "Can you tell us what caused the victim's death in this case?"

"Dr. Hendrix told us a Barghest took Mr. Brook's life in the early morning hours in the DeWitt Clinton Park's dog run." He glanced at the jury. "You can't make this stuff up."

"Detective..." said Sewall.

"Apologies, Your Honor," said Leery, turning to face the judge. "I'm a bit out of practice since coming back from my injuries."

"Yes, well, let's endeavor to keep proper decorum."

"Yes, Your Honor." Leery turned back to Sam and raised his eyebrows.

"And what did the Conjuration, Scrying, and Invocation investigators learn from the victim's dispossessed spirit?"

Leery shrugged his shoulders. "Nothing. Dr. Hendrix said that if the Barghest carried away his soul, it was lost to us."

"I see. And were you able to ascertain if the Barghest did, in fact, carry away his soul?"

Nodding, Leery leaned forward. "Yes. We were able to recapture the Barghest a few nights ago. We sent it back to its home realm, for examination by experts there. Mr. Brook's soul was released to go its own way that very day."

"Thank goodness," said McCoy. "Am I right that Barghests are also called Hell Hounds?"

"That's correct. Just don't say it in front of my partner or her family."

"I'll keep that in mind," said McCoy with a small smile. "And these creatures are called Hell Hounds because they live, where?"

"Gehenna," said Leery.

"Gehenna…otherwise known as Hell in some circles?"

"*Ignorant* circles, maybe," said Leery. "I prefer Gehenna."

"Certainly," said Sam. "I only bring it up to establish that the person who examined the Barghest is an expert in the area of demonology?"

"I'd say so," said Leery.

"And who was that person?"

"Her August Majesty, Agrat bat Mahlat, Sovereign of Demons, Commander of the Eighteen Legions, Queen of the Shabbat, Angel of Divine and Sacred Prostitution, Dancing Roof-Demon, Mistress of Sorcery, One of the Four Queens of Gehenna, She of the Great and Terrible Name."

"I see. Did her brother confirm her findings?"

"Yes."

"And for the sake of the record, who is her brother?"

"Lucifer ben Mahlat, King of Gehenna, Lord of the Flies, Prince of Darkness, Father of Lies, the Great Shaytan, Day-Star, Son of The Morning, Tempter, Angel of Light, Lord of the Air, the Great Adversary, the Roaring Lion, Angel of the Abyss, the Dragon Lord, He of the Great and Terrible Name. And all-around good guy," said Leery.

"Very well. Did Her Majesty learn anything else of interest?"

"Yes, she—"

"Objection, Your Honor," said Laveau without looking up from his notes.

"And what is it, Mr. Laveau?"

"Hearsay."

Sewall bounced his head back and forth on his shoulders for a moment, staring down at the bench. "Given that Mr. McCoy can—and no doubt will—be calling Her Majesty to testify, I'll allow it, subject to such testimony."

"Thank you, Your Honor," said McCoy. He turned back to Leery. "Carry on, Detective."

"She said a warlock had overwritten—corrupted, that is—the original instructions given to the Barghest at the time of his transportation to this realm."

Sam glanced at the jury and smiled. "Could you explain what is meant by that?"

"Sure. See, the Barghest was originally summoned with a poor set of instructions. Basically, it was brought to this realm and left to its own devices."

"Ah. Would it have pursued and dispatched the victim on its own?"

"By the previous set of instructions? No, not according to either the King or Queen of Gehenna."

"Do Their Majesties know what the first set of instructions was?"

"Oh, sure," said Leery. "My partner and I turned up a creep named Bevin Gemble-Croix as part of our initial investigation. Gemble-Croix thought of himself as a high-powered magician back in the days before he knew anything about…well, anything, really. I mean, the guy didn't even know about the Covenancy at the time he muttered his curse. His instructions amounted to: 'Watch Brook and count how many times he sins. When he's sinned enough, get him.' That's paraphrased, of course."

"And this overwriting?"

"Agrat said—oops. Her Majesty told me that a modern warlock modified the instructions to suit his needs. He told the Barghest to seek out Brook and take his soul. No real choice in the matter. It was a magical compulsion."

"I see. Did Her Majesty have any idea if this Gemble-Croix rewrote the instructions himself?"

"She said—"

"Objection, Your Honor," said Laveau, but this time, he looked up. "Her August Majesty is not certified as an expert in Magical Examination to my knowledge."

Sam nodded when Sewall arched an eyebrow at him. "Your Honor, I should hardly think the Witch Queen needs certification. She gave magic to our realm, after all."

Sewall appeared to draw a deep breath. He squinted up at the ceiling, then crossed his arms and looked down at his desk. Finally, he looked up and nodded at McCoy. "Her August Majesty is hereby certified as an expert in the field of magic for the purposes of this trial. Your objection, Mr. Laveau, is overruled."

Sam nodded at Leery.

"Yeah, like I was saying, Her Majesty said the new commands came from a different spellcaster. She could tell because this second caster knew more than just warlockry. She said he also knew wizardry, at least, and likely other arts."

"I see. And does Mr. Gemble-Croix profess knowledge beyond evocation and warlockry?"

"No."

"Very well. Did you have occasion to interview one Lena Cassidy in the course of the investigation?"

"Yes. Several times as a matter of fact."

"What is her connection to the case."

"We first contacted her because she was one of Mr. Brook's ex-girlfriends. She lived close to his Brooklyn home—just a couple of streets over—so we dropped by. We wanted—"

"I see," said McCoy. "Before you go on, did you consider Ms. Cassidy a suspect?"

"No, not at that time."

"But you changed your mind?"

Leery nodded. "Yes. But then we changed it back."

"What did you learn from your first contact with Ms. Cassidy?"

"She didn't know Mr. Brook was dead, for one thing. For another, she really likes pink. She has this piano—"

Sam chuckled. "And was her lack of knowledge about the victim's death enough to rule her out as an initial suspect?"

"No," said Leery. "But the breakup had happened eight or so weeks before, and neither my partner nor myself thought she had the skill to summon the Barghest."

"Very well. What happened next?"

"We discovered a bit of tension in Mr. Brook's firm. That went against what the surviving partners had led us to believe, so we went to talk to them again."

"And did you suspect Mr. Merris at that time?"

Leery grinned with one side of his mouth. "No, he's a slippery one. We suspected the other partner."

"Vastalan Myer—" Sam coughed.

"Yeah, but when he's not around, we call him Myercough to keep from going insane."

"Noted. Why did you suspect Mr. Myercough?"

"His disposition is...well, say he's an acquired taste and leave it at that. Plus, Mr.

Brook had been squirreling away evidence that Myercough was cheating the firm—or at least their clients—on billable hours. We thought that might have been his motive."

"Ah. What did you discover over the course of that meeting?"

"That Ms. Cassidy was the executor of Mr. Brook's will."

Sam turned to the jury and wagged his eyebrows. "This case is a mass of interlinked evidence, isn't it, Detective?"

"I'll say, and, if you'll pardon me for saying so, it's even more complicated by the fact that everyone is a magister."

Sam chuckled. "No offense taken. So, did you return to Ms. Cassidy?"

"Yes."

"Share with us what you learned on that trip."

"For one thing, we learned she likes paintings of naked ladies. For another, she has almost no natural talent for fixing drinks." He smiled. "Not that *we* did any drinking. She had enough for all of us."

McCoy pursed his lips to keep from smiling, but his eyes twinkled. "I meant about the case."

"She admitted she was the executor but hadn't mentioned it on our first trip because we didn't ask. She knew all the sums off the top of her head. You know, who got what and everything. When we pressed her on that, she mentioned the codicil, and that Mr. Merris had brought it over rather than Mr. Brook."

"I see." Sam crossed one arm across his torso and cupped his opposite elbow in his palm, then raised his hand to his lips. "And did she think anything of it? Or of the changes?"

"No, but we did. We asked her why she didn't think it was strange that Brook changed his will so drastically just a few weeks before he died. She made out like a bandit in the new codicil, as did Mr. Merris. We asked her why that didn't raise red flags, and she told us she and Mr. Brook had been talking about getting back together—getting married, in fact."

"Did you find evidence of that at the time?"

"No."

"And since then?"

"Nothing as to the proposal, and nothing originating with Mr. Brook. But we found evidence of numerous calls Mr. Merris made to the Cassidy home."

"Ah. Let's leave that for now. Did you have the chance to question Ms. Cassidy formally?"

"We did. She was very cooperative, and in the end, we released her, convinced she was the defendant's dupe."

"Do you still believe that to be the case?"

"Yeah, even more so since we traced his phone calls."

"What happened next?"

"We went back to Wall Street to pick up Merris for questioning, but the receptionist told us both Mr. Merris and Mr. Myercough had left for the day."

"Did that turn out to be true?" asked Sam.

"No. Merris had left, then come back pretending to be one of Mr. Myercough's clients. He knocked the goblin out and tied him up, then wrought the illusion of Mr. Myercough, which he used to convince everyone the goblin had left the office."

"Good. Now, Detective, can you tell us what happened when you went to Mr. Merris's home?"

"Merris cast the first stone." Leery grinned at the jury, and when no one grinned back, he said, "Well, I guess you had to be there." He shrugged. "The SWAT unit made entry into his home, and then Merris summoned a stone elemental and sicced it on the SWAT guys. It destroyed the entire building getting out, but the servitor warriors with the unit distracted it and eventually subdued it with my partner's help."

"What happened to Merris?"

"He blinked out of the building and tried to get away."

"Blinked?"

"Short-range teleportation. Evidently, it's a wizard thing."

"I see," said McCoy suppressing a smile. "And you gave chase?"

"Sure," said Leery. "I'd changed into my wolf form to try to help the therianthropes, and I tracked his scent, along with a David Kessler, a wolf from the SWAT unit."

"What reason could Mr. Merris have had for summoning the elemental and then running?"

"Simple," said Leery. "He was caught, and he knew it. He wanted to avoid capture and subsequent prosecution."

"Then you believe he showed consciousness of guilt." Sam turned and gave the jury a solemn frown.

"Yes."

"Thank you, Detective. That's all I have, Your Honor."

"Very well. Cross, Mr. Laveau?"

"With relish, Judge Sewall. With relish."

Sewall raised his gaze to the rafters and waved the defense magister on.

"Mr. Oriscoe—"

"That's *Detective* Oriscoe."

"A thousand pardons," said Laveau. "Detective Oriscoe, isn't it true that you and your partner decided early on that Harland Merris was solely responsible for the murder of Richard Brook?"

Leery arched his eyebrows. "Didn't you listen to my testimony? I mean, do you want me to go through all that *again*?"

Laveau flashed a faint smile at him. "Is that a no?"

"Hey, you're sharp."

"I like to think so," said Laveau with a humble grin at the jury. "But didn't you turn your sights on my client with very little in the way of evidence?"

"It was an *investigation*, Mr. Laveau. That's how we cops develop evidence for you to try to get thrown out." He gave the defense magister a wide smile.

Laveau chuckled. "Yes, it is an adversarial system, Detective. I acknowledge we find ourselves on opposite sides quite often. But, getting back to the case at hand, can you please tell the jury why you took Ms. Cassidy into custody, then left her to stew and went back downtown?"

"She was as drunk as a skunk by that time. We needed her to sober up before we interviewed her." He shrugged. "And it was a murder investigation. We try to capture suspects before they know we're on to them."

"But in this case..."

"Like I said, Merris is a slippery one."

"Fine. Can we focus on Ms. Cassidy for a moment or two? Please explain how you ruled her out."

"She cooperated at every step. She didn't invoke her right to representation, she—"

"But she's a magister, isn't she?"

"Yeah. So is your client. So are *you.*"

Laveau's faint smile came back out. "True enough. Do you have an ax to grind with my profession, Detective?"

"Not in general. I like Mr. McCoy and Ms. Carmichael just fine. Oh, and His Honor, of course."

"Of course. But is it fair to say you hold most magisters in a veiled form of contempt?"

"Only the sneaky ones."

"The sneaky ones like Mr. Merris?"

"Hey, if the sneaker fits…"

"Can you explain why you never questioned Mr. Merris in the way you questioned Ms. Cassidy? Why you never gave him a chance to make a deal?"

Leery rocked his head. "Yeah. Ms. Cassidy didn't loose two monsters on the city. She didn't impersonate anyone. When we captured your client, we had him dead to rights. It was decided that we didn't need a confession from him."

"Oh? Who made that determination?"

"I don't know," said Leery. "My boss, Lieutenant Van Helsing, informed me."

"And she didn't say who made the call?"

"Well, she did, but I don't know if it's true."

Laveau smiled at the jury and wagged a finger at Leery. "Who did she say made the call, Detective?"

Leery's lips twitched, and he looked at Sam, but Laveau stepped into his sightline. "Who, Detective?"

"Fine. Van Helsing said Mr. McCoy decided against the interview."

"Thank you. No more questions."

"Hey, don't pretend you just pulled a Perry Mason, Laveau. We don't interview everyone."

"No more questions," repeated Laveau, grinning like the Cheshire cat.

"The witness may step down," said Sewall. "Your next witness, Mr. McCoy?"

Sam glanced over at Geoffrey Laveau and pursed his lips. "Your Honor, I call Bevin Gemble-Croix to the stand."

As the warlock came forward and swore his oath, Laveau frowned down at his hands, clasped white-knuckled on the table before him. Gemble-Croix sat on the edge of the chair in the witness box and frowned out at the courtroom.

"Mr. Gemble-Croix, can you please tell us your profession?" asked Sam as he rose and came over to stand next to the witness box.

"I am a *Magnam Veneficus* of Mot."

"Hmm. What does that mean?"

"*Magnam Veneficus* means 'grand warlock.'"

"Yes, I have a grasp of Latin," said Sam. "What does it mean to a *Magnam Veneficus* in the Temple of Mot?"

Gemble-Croix flashed an arrogant smile at the jury. "For one thing, it means I've succeeded in every challenge Mot has set before me. I have reached the pinnacle of magic. Further, I serve as *Summus Sacerdos* of the Circle of High Priests. I lead the council."

"So, if my rusty Latin is correct, you are the High Priest of the Circle of High Priests?"

The warlock sniffed and picked an imaginary bit of fluff from his trousers.

McCoy smiled. "I'll take that as a 'yes.' Tell me, Mr. Gemble-Croix, were you once a member of the *Sigillum Sanctum Fraternitatis*?"

"I was."

"That same organization also known as the *Arcanum Arcanorum*? The organization founded and originally led by His Honor, Judge Aleister Crowley?"

"Yes," said the warlock with a shrug. "I was a founding member."

"And at that time, were you aware of the larger universe around you?"

"If you mean to inquire if I knew of the Nine Realms and the Covenancy, then my answer must be a qualified no."

"Qualified how?"

"We knew there were other realms, but we could not prove it. We couldn't breach the barriers between this realm and the others, though we did try—and often."

"I see. Did you know Richard Brook, who was also one of the founding members?"

Gemble-Croix's lip curled as he nodded. "A most distasteful man."

"As I understand it, the two of you did not see eye to eye on much."

"Indeed not."

"Did you, after an altercation with Brook, lay a curse on him?"

The warlock pinched the bridge of his nose. "Must we?"

Sam's brow clouded, and he looked down at Gemble-Croix with a fiery gaze. "Yes, sir, this is a murder trial, and we very much must."

"Oh, very well. Yes, I cursed Richard. Or it might be more accurate to say that I *tried* to curse him. I didn't know enough to know what I was doing. I was young."

"But your curse partially succeeded?"

Gemble-Croix sighed. "So I am told. I never saw any sign of such."

"Tell us what you hoped to happen."

"I hoped to call a demon dog to hound Brook to his eternal rest—*unless* Richard mended his ways, in which case the hound would watch him in case he backslid."

"A demon dog?"

"A Hell Hound. A Barghest."

Sam turned and looked at the jury. "But you never saw such a creature?"

"Not at that time."

"And you did not know that summoning succeeded?"

"No. I was not knowledgeable enough—at *that* time—to create adequate control over the beast, so, while it crossed to this realm, it never presented itself in my summoning circle."

"How long ago did all this occur?"

"Three-quarters of a century, give or take a few years."

"And never in the past seventy-five or so years, did you see Richard Brook suffer any sort of ill effects from your curse?"

"None."

"And have you ever met a Ms. Lena Cassidy?"

"No."

"Very well," said Sam, turning to point at the defense table. "One last question, sir. Do you know the man seated at that table?"

Gemble-Croix turned and looked at Harland Merris for the space of several breaths, then turned back to McCoy. "I have never seen that man before in my life. I have no idea who he is, beyond his name in the case on my summons."

"Thank you."

Gemble-Croix did not deign to acknowledge McCoy's thanks, so Sam walked back to the prosecution table and sat down. "I'm finished, Your Honor."

"Mr. Laveau?"

Laveau stood and walked to the witness box, smiling at Gemble-Croix all the while. "Hello, Mr. Gemble-Croix, my name is Geoffrey Laveau."

"Hello."

"Isn't it true, sir, that when you discovered Richard Brook was living high on the hog right under your nose, you became enraged?"

"I knew nothing of Brook in Manhattan until after his death."

"But you did lend your pet Barghest to my client, correct? In order to eliminate your ancient enemy?"

Gemble-Croix sighed. "As I already testified, I didn't know the summoning succeeded and I had no knowledge of Richard Brook's life here in the City."

"Pardon my disbelief, but I find that impossible to believe."

"And I find it hard to care."

Laveau smiled and gave the jury a humble look. "In Mr. McCoy's examination of you a few moments ago, he asked if you'd ever seen a Barghest, and you responded, 'Not at that time.'"

"Yes."

"I take it, then, that you've seen a Barghest since that time?"

"Of course, I'm the *Magnam Veneficus* of Mot."

"So, you *have* successfully summoned Hell Hounds?"

"Yes, and *lawfully*. What of it?"

"Isn't it true that you summoned such a creature for my client *illegally*? That you tasked him with directing the creature to attack Richard Brook?"

Gemble-Croix sighed and shook his head. "I've never met your wretched client, sir. I've never spoken to him. I've certainly never entered into a conspiracy with him."

"So you say, Mr. Gemble-Croix. Are you sure you want to take that position?"

The warlock rolled his eyes. "Quite sure."

"Very well. Your Honor, I have no more questions at this time, but I would like to notify the Court that I'll be adding a rebuttal witness to my list."

"Very well," said Sewall. "Mr. Gemble-Croix, you may step down. You will make yourself available should we need to recall you."

Gemble-Croix grimaced and shook his head as he left the room.

"Mr. McCoy?"

"Thank you, Your Honor. The People call Her August Majesty, Agrat bat Mahlat."

"Your Honor!" said Laveau, leaping to his feet. "That infringes on the Covenant of Sovereign Privilege."

"Your Honor, I have not compelled Her Majesty's testimony. She volunteered it."

"I see," said Sewall. "Overruled, Mr. Laveau. Woody, make sure Her Majesty is comfortable. All rise!" Even Judge Sewall assumed a standing position.

The wooden-faced bailiff nodded and went to fetch the Queen of Gehenna. When he returned, he preceded a sable-haired beauty wearing a long sequined gown the color of blood, bejeweled with blood garnets and orange sapphires. A hush fell over the courtroom, and one of the men on the jury went so far as to gasp. Agrat glanced at him and smiled, then took her place in the witness box.

Sam bowed at the waist. "Your Majesty, thank you for offering your testimony in this case."

"It's no problem," she said.

"Your Majesty," said Judge Sewall. "I feel compelled to remind you that you are under no obligation to testify here. The Covenant of Sovereign Privilege allows you to refuse."

"Thank you. I am aware."

"Very well. Proceed, Mr. McCoy."

"Thank you, Your Honor." McCoy came around the prosecution table and approached to within a few steps of the witness box. "Could you start by sharing your title with the jury?"

She smiled at the jurors. "Of course. I am Agrat bat Mahlat, Sovereign of Demons, Commander of the Eighteen Legions, Queen of the Shabbat, Angel of Divine and Sacred Prostitution, Dancing Roof-Demon, Mistress of Sorcery, One of the Four Queens of Gehenna, She of the Great and Terrible Name."

"Mistress of Sorcery—is the title honorary?"

"No, Mr. McCoy. I gave magic to your realm when I introduced Amemar the Sage to its workings."

"Then you are not limited to what we, in this realm, have come to define as sorcery? The communication with spirits and other-realm entities for the purposes of augury?"

"No, in this case, the term applies to the broader definition. Simply put, magic."

"I see. Thank you for indulging my curiosity, Your Majesty. How were you made aware of this case?"

"My daughter and her partner were the primary investigators."

"Your daughter, known as Dru Nogan in this realm?"

"Yes, and her charming partner, Leery Oriscoe."

Sam grinned. "And what is your daughter's name in Gehenna?"

"Drusilla bat Agrat bat Mahlat, Crown Princess, Heir to the Throne of Gehenna, She of the Great and Terrible Name." She shrugged and smiled at the jury. "She'll acquire more titles as time goes on."

"Did you take a special interest in the Barghest running loose in Manhattan?"

"I did," said Agrat. "I *am* the Sovereign of Demons, after all, and while a Barghest may not be a fully sentient demon, they are denizens of Gehenna and are given the same rights and privileges as everyone else."

"Most enlightened, Your Majesty. We heard earlier testimony that you examined the Barghest after it was retrieved from this realm?"

Agrat nodded. "Yes. Dru and Leery sent the poor creature home to me. The Barghest was in a state of confusion due to the manipulation it suffered at the hands of this fool"—she flung her hand toward Merris—"and the fool who summoned him in the first place."

"How are you sure the defendant manipulated the hound?"

"I don't like that term," she said. "The *Barghest* bore traces of his mistreatment. Each spell leaves a trace—most citizens of the Covenancy know that. With a summoned creature, one would expect pure warlockry, but that was not the case here."

"Ah, I see. And what did the traces on the Barghest show?"

"A unique combination of various disciplines. Warlockry, certainly, but also wizardry, witchcraft, alchemy, and invocation. There were others, but the traces were so thin I could not determine specifics."

"Did these traces lead you to any particular individual?"

Agrat laughed. "I've already said. That man." She pointed at Merris again. "Everything about him screams 'match,' even as he sits there trying to look innocent."

McCoy nodded and turned to look at Merris. "We've been told Mr. Merris is skilled at impersonation. Is there any chance some other person skilled in the art might have cast the spell and made it look like Mr. Merris did the deed?"

"If it were someone other than me doing the examination, possibly." She lifted her shoulders. "As things stand, no."

"You sound certain, Your Majesty."

"I am, Mr. McCoy." She turned and glared at Merris, and the temperature in the room rose ten degrees. "His Majesty, my royal brother, agrees. He bade me tell the defendant that the two of them shall speak of the matter at some future point."

Sam raised his eyebrows and looked at the jury. "I certainly wouldn't want to be in the defendant's shoes."

"Your Honor, I object!" said Laveau.

"Your grounds, sir?"

"Uh... Improper characterization?"

Sewall sighed. "Her Majesty answered the question asked, which had nothing to do with your client's character. Sit down, Mr. Laveau."

"Yes, Your Honor."

Sewall motioned for Sam to continue.

"One last question, Your Majesty. Did you find any evidence on the Barghest of a conspiracy between the original summoner, the defendant, or any other person?"

"No, Mr. McCoy. The Barghest was set free through incompetence the better part of a century ago. This man"—she pointed at Harland Merris—"began to co-opt the Barghest less than a year ago, moving slowly and with great caution, and he finally gave it instructions to kill Mr. Brook a few hours before the murder. No other person interfered."

"Thank you, Your Majesty."

"A pleasure, Mr. McCoy," Agrat said in a sultry voice that left Sam short on breath. "Maybe we'll see one another again."

Sam bowed to cover the urge to gulp, then returned to his seat.

"Mr. Laveau?"

"Yes, thank you, Your Honor." Geoffrey Laveau got to his feet and came toward the witness box, but as Agrat raised her gaze to his, he stumbled to a stop. "Uh... Your Majesty, could you please tell the Court where you received your degree in Magical Examination?"

"I have none."

"Oh. I must have misunderstood. Then, please tell us where you studied for your advanced degrees?"

She cocked her head to the side. "None."

"Hmm. And yet you profess to be an expert in all forms of magic?"

Agrat nodded, narrowing her eyes.

"It's an empty boast, isn't it?"

A lopsided smile creased Agrat's face. "Do I need to spell 'Mistress of Sorcery?'"

"No, I understand the implication. My questions go to where this title of yours came from?"

"I have explained that."

"Your pardon, Your Majesty, but as I understood your testimony, you received the title for the act of giving magic to some sage in ancient history?"

"Yes, that is correct."

"And before you did that, did magic exist?"

"Not in this realm."

"But elsewhere?"

Agrat rolled her eyes and treated the jury to a longsuffering smile. "Of course, Mr. Laveau."

"Ah. Then you didn't invent it?"

Moving slowly and with great precision, Agrat turned her fierce gaze on Laveau. "No one 'invented' magic. It is a fundamental force in the multiverse."

Laveau frowned and sucked his teeth. "Tell me again why your so-called expertise in magic is credible."

"Mr. Laveau!" snapped Sewall. "Decorum, sir!"

But Agrat only smiled. "How old are you, Mr. Laveau?"

"I don't see—"

"*How old are you?*" Agrat said, leaning forward and pinning him with her hot gaze.

"Thirty-seven."

"A mere babe. My expertise, young one, comes from more than a thousand times as many years of practice and study." As she spoke, Agrat's voice dropped in timbre while increasing in volume. "My expertise comes from witnessing millions of incantations, making millions of cantrips, invocations, and evocations." A hot tempest wind swirled through the courtroom. "My family has been using magic since before your realm used fire." The lights flickered, making shadows that leaped and danced like cavorting demons. "Magic to me is as air is to you. It sustains me; it gives me succor." The color of her dress dimmed, and her flesh turned gray. "If you like, sir, I can arrange a demonstration of my expertise for you." She became a thing of liquid black smoke on the last word, all except her vermillion-glowing eyes.

Laveau swallowed hard. "I-I-I..." He forced his mouth shut, sniffed, and tore his gaze away from her eyes. "That won't be necessary, Your Majesty. I withdraw the question."

"As you wish," said Agrat, and the lights steadied, the wind died, her dress was once again red, and her flesh pale as cream.

Laveau stood there gawping at her innocent smile, then he blinked several times, turned, and almost ran back to his seat. "No more questions, Your Honor."

"I should think not," said the judge in a mild tone. He turned to Agrat and bowed his head. "Thank you, Your Majesty. Most illuminating. You may step down."

"My pleasure, Judge Sewall."

She stood with a dancer's grace and walked toward the gate in the bar. She stopped next to the defense table but didn't look down at Laveau or Merris. Instead, she tapped the table with one long, scarlet fingernail, then went on her way.

9

After the lunch break, Sam presented the rest of his case—the testimony of Glisandra, the receptionist at Brook, Merris, and Myercough, and the testimony of Lena Cassidy. Afterward, he rested the prosecution's case against Harland Merris and sank into his chair.

"What's the matter?" Angie whispered. "Did all this afternoon's fluff exhaust you?"

Sam grinned and nodded. "That and the bacon cheeseburger I had for lunch."

"Mr. Laveau, are you ready to present your defense?" asked Judge Sewall?

"Judge, I must request a continuance."

"I've already given you one, Mr. Laveau."

"But, Your Honor, I need time to find a witness."

Sam scowled, as did Sewall. "What witness? Woody tells me you have a witness waiting."

"Yes, but not the right one."

Sewall hooked his finger at Laveau. "Come here, young man. You, too, Mr. McCoy."

Sam smiled and approached the bench.

"What's this foolishness, Mr. Laveau?" demanded the judge.

"My rebuttal witness, Your Honor. I need time to find him."

"And the goblin in the witness room?"

Sam arched an eyebrow at Laveau. "That's Vastalan Myercough, Judge. He's here as a character witness."

"Your Honor, Mr. Myercough is one of Richard Brook's beneficiaries, and a victim of the crime. He was also the original magister of record. Any testimony—"

"I remember, Mr. McCoy, but Mr. Laveau can call anyone he wishes, even witnesses who are terrible for his case. Who is this rebuttal witness?"

"A member of the Temple of Mot, Your Honor. He can testify that Bevin Gemble-Croix did, in fact, meet my client at the temple. Further, he—"

"Your Honor, the People will stipulate that Gemble-Croix might have known the defendant in his capacity with the Temple of Mot. It's hardly earth-shattering testimony."

"No, Mr. McCoy, it isn't. Well, Mr. Laveau? Is Mr. McCoy's stipulation enough for you?"

"No, Your Honor. My witness will definitively put Gemble-Croix and my client together in several workrooms of the temple. They did magic together, Your Honor, and I can prove it."

"How many people were in the room?" asked Sam.

"What?"

"How many other Motian practitioners were in these workrooms at the same time as Mr. Gemble-Croix and the defendant?"

"Several, but what does—"

"The People stipulate that Gemble-Croix and Merris performed group rituals and spells in the Temple of Mot, Your Honor."

"I can't see the necessity of waiting for a witness of such nebulous testimony, Mr. Laveau. Can your witness say Gemble-Croix and the defendant *spoke* to one another?"

Laveau hung his head. "They might have."

"Ah. They might not have, with equal probability. Your motion for a continuance is denied. Step back and move on with your case, sir."

"But, Your Honor!"

Sewall pointed at the defense table and glared at Laveau until he turned and walked back to his seat.

"Your Honor, the defense calls Vastalan Myercough." Merris tugged at his elbow, and Laveau bent down. "I apologize, Your Honor. I call Vastalan Myer—" He coughed.

Shaking his head, Sewall waved the bailiff toward the witness room and waited while the goblin made his oath to tell the truth.

Laveau walked forward eagerly and said, "Hello, Mr. Myer"—he coughed—"did I say that right?"

Myercough nodded but narrowed his eyes.

"Tell me about your partner, Harland Merris."

"Likable fellow, for a human," said Myercough. "He works hard, keeps his workplace clean, and rarely interrupts."

"That's great, but does he have it in him to mastermind the death of your other partner, Richard Brook?"

Vastalan scoffed. "Hardly. He's a follower, not a leader. If Harland did this thing, he was led to it by a woman or a personage of power."

"And you can see no instance when Mr. Merris might—"

"No!" snapped the goblin. "Come, come, don't make me repeat myself! I'm a busy man, sir! Busy!"

"Uh, yes. You are a beneficiary of the victim's will, are you not?"

"Yes. His true will, that is."

"And you stand to grow rich once the will is settled?"

"I'm already rich, you fool!"

"Uh, yes. Are you sure *you* didn't arrange Mr. Brook's death?"

"Your Honor!" cried Sam. "This is accusation by ambush!"

"Oh, I don't mind," said Myercough. "I'm a goblin. I'm used to people thinking the worst of me."

"Mr. Laveau, I'd like to remind you that this is *your* witness. But the witness may answer."

"No," said Vastalan. "I did not murder Richard. I liked Richard. He was good at arguing and good at maintaining an interoffice war. It made things...fun."

"I see," said Laveau, frowning at his shoes. "Why should we believe your denial?"

"Don't, if you like," said Myercough. "I really don't care. But before you make your accusation official, I'd ask you to present your so-called proof."

Laveau turned away.

"That's what I thought," said Myercough.

"Let's return to Mr. Merris. What—"

"I've already answered your questions. How many ways can I say, 'he's too stupid to have done this?'"

Merris leaned forward, his gaze burning. "Too stupid?" he hissed.

"Control your client, Mr. Laveau."

"Yes, Your Honor. Nothing more, Your Honor."

"Mr. McCoy?"

"Just a few questions, Judge Sewall."

"Proceed."

"Were you attacked by the defendant at your workplace?"

"Attack is a strong term."

McCoy grinned. "Okay. What would you call it?"

Myercough rolled his gaze skyward. "A subduing."

"Fine. Did Mr. Merris subdue you in your office, then usurp your identity?"

"He did create an illusion of me and made it walk out of the building."

"To what end?"

"I suppose to throw off the police. To make it seem as if I had something to do with the crimes, perhaps."

"Did you, as Mr. Laveau alleges?"

"No!"

Sam nodded to the goblin magister. "We've heard your testimony that you are a beneficiary in Mr. Brook's will. Why hasn't the will been executed?"

"That fool magister of Brook's has frozen the proceedings until this mess is resolved, and there's the matter of *your* injunction against disbursing the funds, as well."

"I see. Are you testifying here today to try to alleviate those blockages? Say as part of a conspiracy to help Mr. Merris win an acquittal? Perhaps…Mr. Merris might withdraw the false codicil? Would that influence your testimony?"

"What?" Myercough blushed furiously. "No!"

"I see," said McCoy with a grin. "Nothing more."

"The witness may step down." Sewall looked at Laveau and arched an eyebrow.

"Your Honor, the defense rests."

"Then I'm ready to hear closing arguments," said Sewall.

Laveau nodded, but his shoulders slumped, and he didn't raise his gaze from the floor. "Ladies and gentlemen of the jury, part and parcel with our system of justice is the concept that the Locus must prove its case beyond a reasonable shadow of a doubt. I submit that they haven't done so in this case. My cross-examination of Gemble-Croix, and the subsequent stipulation by the prosecutor that he gave false testimony—"

"Your Honor!" cried Sam.

"You can rebut in your closing, Mr. Prosecutor."

"—provides one such shadow. His partner, who is a victim of the fraud and impersonation charges, came today to offer his testimony as to the defendant's character—another shadow. What else have the People shown you? The testimony of police officers who'd already decided my client was the sole perpetrator. The Witch Queen's testimony about the so-called magical residues found on some Barghest? Have the people even proven that it was *the* Barghest who took Richard Brook's life? No. For these reasons, you *must* find my client not guilty of these charges." He turned and shuffled to his chair, then sat without looking at anyone.

McCoy turned in his chair and stared at Laveau for a moment, then shook his head and stood. He turned to the jury and smiled. "I believe Mr. Laveau's closing argument might be the most creative use of self-deception I've ever seen. The People did not stipulate that Bevin Gemble-Croix gave false testimony—just that he may have, at some point in the past, conducted group rituals in his role at the Temple of Mot that Mr. Merris took part in. Further…" He shook his head. "No, never mind. Look, I'll make this simple for you. If you have any doubt that Mr. Merris committed the crimes as we've described, find him not guilty. But"—he held up his index finger—"if you find the testimony of one of NYPD's most decorated detectives believable, if you find Her Majesty, Agrat bat Mahlat, to be credible, and if you believe *our* theory of the events presented, find Mr. Merris guilty." He gave them a short bow, then turned and bowed his head to Judge Sewall. "Thank you, Your Honor, and ladies and gentlemen of the jury, for your kind attentions."

CHAPTER 4

THE VERDICT

I

The jury took only thirty-five minutes to reach a verdict, and Judge Sewall recalled everyone before most had left the building. The jury was stone-faced as they re-entered the courtroom.

Judge Sewall turned to the jury box, a stern expression on his face. "Mr. Foreman, you have reached a conclusion so quickly?"

"We have, Judge."

"I see. Have you considered all the evidence in the case? Are you satisfied your verdict is both just and fair?"

"Yes, Your Honor—to both questions."

"Very well. Mr. Foreman, in the matter of the People versus Harland Merris, on the counts of impersonation of a magical entity, how do you find?"

"We find the defendant guilty, Your Honor."

"I accept your finding. On the count of fraud against the court, how do you find?"

"Guilty, Judge."

"Very well. On the two counts of summoning other-realm entities without a license?"

"We find the defendant guilty."

"Now, Mr. Foreman, for this last charge, I must ask you again if you have paid attention to the instructions I gave, and if you have considered all the evidence impartially and come to a conclusion that all members of the jury support?"

"We have, Your Honor."

"Very well. On the count of magical murder in the first degree, how do you find?"

The jury foreman turned and stared at Harland Merris. "We find him guilty, Your Honor."

"I instruct the clerk to record the jury's findings and enter a verdict of guilty on all counts. If there is no objection, I am ready to pass sentence in the interest of justice."

Sam nodded. "The People do not object."

Laveau stared down at his feet.

"Mr. Laveau? Do you have an objection?"

"Would it matter if I did?"

"I will consider that a 'no,' sir." The judge fixed Harland Merris with a steely glare. "Harland Merris, having been found guilty on all counts by a jury of your peers, I hereby sentence you to two terms of twenty years for the impersonation charges. On the charge of defrauding the court, I sentence you to the maximum allowable by law, which is ten years, and I chastise you, sir. I wish I could sentence you to the pillory, but alas, those days are over. On the two counts of summoning other-realm entities without a license, I sentence you to two years each count. Finally, on the charge of magical murder in the first degree, I sentence you to a lifetime in the dungeons of the Locus of New York." He picked up his gavel. "I am disgusted with you, sir. I hope this time is enough for you to realize the scope and depth of your crimes, that you find meaningful reform as you serve your sentences. Have you anything to say?"

Merris shook his head but then said, "He killed my sister, Your Honor. It was an accident, maybe, a mistake, but he killed her, and he deserved to pay for his crime."

"As do you, sir. As do you." Sewall banged his gavel and disappeared.

CHAPTER 5

THE END

I

Leery and Dru walked up the aisle in the gallery and stood across the bar from McCoy. "Way to go, Counselor," said Leery and thumped Sam on the back.

"Hey! What about me?" asked Angie.

"You did good, too," said Leery.

Sam glanced across at Laveau who still sat at the defense table, his gaze down, shoulders slumped. "Excuse me a moment." He crossed the aisle and tapped the table in unconscious mimicry of Agrat.

"Here to gloat?" croaked Laveau.

"No," said Sam. "This was a hard case, Laveau, but you could have done better."

"Sure. Why not heap it on?"

"There were strategies you could have tried, avenues you didn't explore."

"I can't help that I'm not as good a magister as you, McCoy."

"You aren't," said Sam. "But you could be if you applied yourself."

"Right," sneered Laveau. "You with your fancy Unicorn-horn League education, and poor Geoff Laveau with his cheap night school degree."

Sam turned back to the prosecution table and grabbed his briefcase. "Come on," he said to Angie and the others. "I need a drink."

As they left the courtroom, Leery leaned close. "Why didn't you tell him?"

"Tell him what?" asked Angie.

"That your boss, here, went to Queens College."

"I didn't want to break up his party," said Sam.

"His party?"

Sam grinned sourly. "A party of one. Self-pity." He looked Leery up and down. "Are you well enough for a scotch?"

"Hey, if you're buying, I'm well enough."

Dru shook her head and bumped him with her shoulder. "He'll have coffee." She held up a finger. "*One* coffee. In a cup."

"Aw. You're no fun."

"Wanna bet?" she asked, eyes twinkling, and she bumped him with her shoulder once more.

I hope you've enjoyed this episode of CLAW & WARDER and are chomping at the bit to get on to the next. *Slay Fell Things: CLAW & WARDER Episode 9* can be found here: https://ehv4.us/4cw9.

If you've enjoyed this novel, please consider joining my Readers Group by visiting https://ehv4.us/join. Or follow me on BookBub by visiting my profile page there: https://ehv4.us/bbub.

For my complete bibliography, please visit: https://ehv4.us/bib.

Books these days succeed or fail based on the strength of their reviews. I hope you will consider leaving a review—as an independent author, I could use your help. It's easy (I promise). You can leave your review by clicking on this link: https://ehv4.us/2revcw8

AUTHOR'S NOTE

Hello there! I'm glad to see you. We're almost there, my friend, almost to the last episode of CLAW & WARDER I have planned for 2020. I had a lot of fun (and some of it unexpected) writing this penultimate episode, but there's even more in store in *Slay Fell Things: CLAW & WARDER Episode 9*.

Even so, I must admit, I'm tired. Not with the series—I *love* writing these books—but mentally and physically, I'm out of gas. I still have more writing that I've committed to for this year (I will get all that done, so rest easy), but Petunia the Wimpy (my illness) hasn't made keeping the schedule an easy thing. I've spent most of the year (since February) without an effective medication, and that's taken its toll. Funny thing—I start my third trial tonight—in about twenty minutes, as a matter of fact, so fingers crossed.

Someone asked me recently how I manage to avoid letting my illness derail my productivity. It struck me as strange because, to me, my productivity *has* decreased. I've struggled with a few deadlines, *Wrath Child* has taken a lot more energy and time than it should have, and I haven't spent as much time running the giant machine that powers Oz as I would have otherwise. All of that is down to Petunia.

One of the things I wrote and deleted about ten times on the blog is about something I call "Grief Days." There are days when the devastation this illness has wrought in my life overwhelms me. It's very much like the scene in *Errant Gods* where Hank wakes up and everything seems too much, bleak, horrible. Grief Days are hard. I feel as though I'm on the edge of breaking down (and often do for the silliest reasons). My Viking side calls those days self-pity, but I realized something this year: it's not self-pity. It's *grief*, hence the name. It's grieving the loss of my healthy self, of my plans, my aspirations, of time with my family, of friendships, of the ability to do things I took for granted, and of being the strongest guy in the room (most of the time). Melissa said it best in an interview. To paraphrase: when you're dealing with RA, it's often about what we *can't* do. So, these feelings are grief, and, in my humble opinion, grieving is necessary.

It's okay to grieve what your Personal Monster™ has taken from you. It's okay to grieve the loss of your health, your hobbies, and your self-image.

But it's important to grieve and move on. Again, I'm going to paraphrase my wonderful wife, my Supergirl: it's important to try to appreciate what we *can* do.

Here's what I *can* do. I can continue to write. I will continue to write. But the pace may slow, depending on whether I can find a good medication that knocks Petunia upside the head with a hammer. I've got the same big plans for next year—too many series ideas, too many things I want to write. Petunia has the same plans as always, too, but will not win. I won't abide it.

So, stick around, my friend. Head on over to Facebook, if you haven't already, and join us (https://ehv4.us/fbog). Drop by and put your feet up. Grieve if you need to, we understand. Then, laugh with us, have fun with us, join the family. We're here, and you're welcome.

ABOUT THE AUTHOR

Erik Henry Vick is an author of dark speculative fiction who writes despite a disability caused by his Personal Monster™ (also known as an autoimmune disease.) He writes to hang on to the few remaining shreds of his sanity.

He lives in Western New York with his wife, Supergirl; their son; a Rottweiler named after a god of thunder; and two extremely psychotic cats. He fights his Personal Monster™ daily with humor, pain medicine, and funny T-shirts.

Erik has a B.A. in Psychology, an M.S.C.S., and a Ph.D. in Artificial Intelligence. He has worked as a criminal investigator for a state agency, a college professor, a C.T.O. for an international software company, and a video game developer.

He'd love to hear from you on social media:

    Blog: https://erikhenryvick.com
    Twitter: https://twitter.com/BerserkErik
    Facebook: https://fb.me/erikhenryvick
    Amazon author pages:
        USA: https://ehv4.us/amausa
        UK: https://ehv4.us/amauk
    Goodreads Author Page: https://ehv4.us/gr
    BookBub Author Profile: http://ehv4.us/bbub

Made in the USA
Monee, IL
29 January 2023